CW00796623

THE
INDIFFERENCE OF
HEAVEN

THE INDIFFERENCE OF HEAVEN

By

Michael Allen Rose

Omnium Gatherum
Los Angeles

The Indifference of Heaven
Copyright © 2018 Michael Allen Rose
ISBN-13: 9781949054996
ISBN-10: 1949054993

All rights reserved. No part of this book may be reproduced or
transmitted in any form or by any electronic or mechanical means,
including photocopying, recording or by any information storage and
retrieval system, without the written permission of the author and
publisher omniumgatherumedia.com.

This book is a work of fiction. Names, characters, places and
incidents are either the products of the author's imagination or are
used fictitiously. Any resemblance to actual events or persons, living
or dead, is coincidental.

First Edition

Special Graffiti Thanks

The instances of graffiti used in this story come from real world examples of public bathroom graffiti that actually exist in our reality. These were captured by a multitude of people from geographically diverse locations and provided to the author for artistic purposes. Thank you to the following providers:

o   Sauda Namir
o   Jeremy Robert Johnson
o   Jess Gulbranson
o   Mark Allen Berryhill
o   Liv Rainey-Smith
o   Shane Cartledge
o   Jeff Burk
o   Cody Goodfellow
o   Eric Hendrixson

Special thanks to Cameron Pierce, Sauda Namir and Kirsten Alene for the wonderful conversation that led to this story, and a special thank you to Danger Slater for his support and assistance in the process of writing this.

— DAY 1—

My name is George Patroklos. I'm the owner of the Duffle-bag Tap. I opened this place more than ten years ago with my own money. We're a neighborhood bar, lots of regulars, a few random college kids stopping through on what they call dive crawls, one or two long time bar flies, and the occasional Mexican dude selling tamales bar to bar. My patrons get hungry, and we don't have kitchen service anymore.

Too much trouble.

I'm writing all this down so there's a record of the crimes perpetrated against me and my bar, and I want to make sure that if it comes to something, I have evidence to slap down on the precinct desk, so I can show what happened. I got a good memory, but there's just too much here to keep inside my skull, so enter this diary, or crime blotter, or captain's log, or whatever you want to call it.

The first time I noticed the writing was Monday morning, but I didn't really think about it too much. Once in a while, some drunk asshole will scrawl something in the bathroom when he goes to pop the cork. It's part of the cost of doing business in an industry where you get people stupid out of their minds sometimes. Sometimes, some of the shit I see in there is actually pretty funny. There are a couple of scrawls in there that I haven't cleaned up because they make me laugh, and from all reports, they make my patrons laugh too. Sometimes, someone will mention one of them.

One of my favorites, someone carved into the condom dispenser with a pocket knife:

This is the worst gum I ever chewed

I don't want to come off as some asshole without a sense of humor. I keep the bar clean and organized, but you know, people are going to do stupid things when they're drunk, and as long as it's little things, I guess I don't feel like it's too harmful. In a way, it gives the place character.

So, the writing I'm talking about—the stuff I glance at and then promptly forget on Monday morning—this is different. Somebody has taken up almost the whole stall door. Looks like they'd been in there a long while. Of course, I don't keep track of my patrons' bathroom habits, so I didn't notice anyone spending a particularly long time in there, but they must have. This was sentences, paragraphs, all the way down. I was pretty pissed off, but I didn't pay a lot of attention to what it said. I go and grab a couple of bar rags from the utility closet and spray it down with bleach water and scrape it all off. I guess it must have been ink, or something, but thankfully not one of those Sharpie permanent markers, so I don't have to re-paint the door.

Tuesday morning, same deal. I walk into the men's restroom, and I check the stalls, like I do every morning, and sure enough, the same stall door has a bunch of lettering all the way from top to bottom. I have to think for a second, whether or not I'd actually cleaned it up the day before, or if I'd had some kind of weird dream, but no, I was sure I did. So, I do it again. I scrub the hell out of that door, cursing up a storm, but it all came off pretty good, so I guess I figure, no real harm done.

This morning, Wednesday, it's back again.

So now, I'm pissed. I get my rag and spray the hell out of the surface and start wiping, but as I'm doing it, I have this moment where I catch something out of the corner of my eye, I guess, so I stop for a second and breathe.

Whoever was doing this shit picked up right where they left off. Same penmanship, everything. You know how sometimes there's this funny feeling in your head, where something just isn't right? Intuition, maybe. Or a kind of sixth sense? Well, I pick up on something weird just then. My eyes kind of focus in like a camera lens on a few distinct words, so I take a closer look, and that's when I see that it's about a fight. These sentences sound like they came right straight out of somebody's confession to the police.

I figure before I scrub this shit off the wall, I should write it down for the cops, or whoever, in case this keeps happening, or in case some nut is coming in here talking about his crimes or some awful thing. I don't really want to take the time to jot it all down, but if some asshole's going to keep wrecking my stall walls, I guess I have no choice. Unfortunately, I'd wiped some of the bottom part off before I got clear to seeing my way forward, so this is as much of what was there this morning as I could write down. Hopefully this is the last time, and ultimately, I'm doing this for nothing:

WE WERE SKIPPING STONES ALONG THE RIVER. THE POLLUTION IN THE WATER GAVE EACH THROW EXTRA LIFT AS THE FLAT ROCKS WHISKED ACROSS THE SURFACE ONLY TO SINK INTO A VORTEX OF OILY RIPPLES. WE TRIED TO IGNORE THE SMELL OF ROTTING

FISH ON THE BANKS, BUT IT FOLDED ITSELF INTO THE WRINKLES AND QUARRIES OF OUR FLESH LIKE A PARASITIC MIASMA.

THERE WERE JUST THE TWO OF US TODAY, DONNIE AND I, BASKING IN THIS ENDLESS SUMMER. OUR USUAL GANG OF FRIENDS AND HANGERS-ON WERE SCATTERED ELSEWHERE, SUMMER SCHOOL FOR THE SLOWER ONES, SUMMER JOBS FOR THE OLDER ONES, BUT DONNIE AND I HAD NOTHING BETTER TO DO THAN JUST BE, HERE AND NOW. AT LEAST, THAT'S HOW I SAW IT. THE LACK OF RESPONSIBILITIES AND THE HAZY HEAT OF JULY MARKED

OUR DAYS WITH AN INTRICATE SERIES OF MOMENTS THAT FIT TOGETHER LIKE PIECES OF A BROKEN PUZZLE BOX. THE TREE-LINED RIVER BANK WAS A FREQUENT DESTINATION IN THE QUEST TO RELIEVE OUR BOREDOM AND ESCAPE THE OPPRESSIVE RAYS OF THE SUN. MOST ADULTS AVOIDED THE RIVER, AND DISPENSED ADVICE TO THAT EFFECT TO ANY YOUNGSTER WITHIN EARSHOT. THERE WERE A WHOLE SLEW OF FACTORIES, SLAUGHTERHOUSES AND REFINERIES UPRIVER THAT HAD SLOWLY POISONED THE WATERS AND GIVEN THEM A SHEEN OF MERCURY SMOOTH AND PHOSPHORESCENT GLEAM.

WE KNEW BETTER THAN TO DRINK FROM IT, BUT THE OFFICIAL WORD WAS THAT SWIMMING AND BOATING WERE OKAY, DEPENDING ON THE FLOW AND THE TIME OF SEASON. MOST AFTERNOONS, KIDS WOULD LINE THE SHORES, PRACTICING THEIR ROCK THROWS AT PASSING FLOTSAM, SWINGING OFF ROPESANDGENERALLYBEING A DANGER TO THEMSELVES IN ONLY THE WAY THAT YOUTH UNENCUMBERED BY EXPERIENCE CAN.

THATDAYINPARTICULAR, THE CLOUDS HAD NESTLED IN, A COOL BLANKET SHIELDING US FROM THE SUN. A SOUTHERN

WIND BLEW HOT ACROSS OUR BACKS AS WE CONTINUED LOOKING FOR THE PERFECT LAUNCHING PAD. DONNIE WAS WALKING AHEAD OF ME BY HERSELF. SHE KICKED AT A LARGE BEETLE WITH THE TOE OF HER SANDAL. IT SCURRIED AWAY AND SLIPPED UNDER A LARGE FLAT ROCK MARKING THE EDGE OF A WEEDY GROUPING OF GRASSY STALKS.

INSTEAD OF THE PEACEFUL CALM USUALLY PRESENT HERE, MY HEAD WAS FILLED WITH NOISE. EVERYTHING HAD BEEN WELLING UP, TUMBLING AROUND AND MAKING THINGS FUZZY. FOR

THE FIRST TIME SINCE I'D KNOWN HER, DONNIE LOOKED BORED. HER POSTURE WAS SLUMPED, BUT HER LIMBS FRANTICALLY TWITCHED WITH THE DESIRE TO RUN OFF AND DO SOMETHING ELSE, SOMETHING MORE IMPORTANT. SHE WASN'T LOOKING AT ME, BUT MORE IMPORTANTLY, NO PART OF HER WAS HERE. SHE WAS WITH ME, AND YET I WAS ALONE. "HAVING FUN?" HER ANSWER WAS A MURMUR, THE SOUND OF FALLING LEAVES, AND SUDDENLY MY FACE FLUSHED HOT. MY SKIN WAS ON FIRE, AND I NEEDED SOMETHING TO COOL IT. MY EYES SQUINTED AND BURNED, AS THE CLOUDS SEEMED TO

SPEED ACROSS THE SKY LIKE MISSHAPEN TRAFFIC ON AN UPSIDE DOWN EXPRESSWAY.

I STARED HOLES INTO DONNIE'S BACK. SHE MUMBLED SOMETHING LIKE "IT'S NICE, ISN'T IT?" TRYING TO MAKE AN EFFORT TO BE, PROJECTING DEFLATED HOPES INTO THE RUNNING WATER. A FEW BRANCHES FLOATED BY, CRASHING AGAINST EACH OTHER LIKE BOATS TRYING TO CAPSIZE THEIR RIVALS IN A RACE. A DEEP BLUE ECHO OF THE SKY CASCADED ACROSS THE SURFACE OF THE WATER AS A PART APPEARED IN THE CLOUDS. STRIATIONS

SEPARATEDEACHCLOUDINTO
A BEAM OF SMOKY LIGHT AS I
LEAPT ATOP DONNIE. I FELT
HER KNEES BUCKLE, AND WE
BOTH WENT DOWN INTO THE
RIVER, A STAGNANT SPLASH
AND A SCREAM OF RAGE AND
SURPRISE PINPOINTING OUR
POSITION AND FOCUSING THE
HEAT INSIDE MY HEAD TO A
FINE LASER POINT.

I LANDED OFF BALANCE AND
FELL TO MY LEFT AS SHE
ROLLED OUT FROM UNDER ME,
SLAPPING THE SURFACE OF
THE WATER INTO A RIPPLED
FRENZY. SHE KICKED HER
LEGS OUT AND CAUGHT ME IN
THE SIDE, NEAR MY KIDNEYS.
I FELT DIZZY FOR A MOMENT,

AND THE BILE ROSE UP IN MY THROAT. UNDETERRED, I CRAWLED FORWARD MADLY, SKITTERING LIKE A SPIDER, AND STRADDLED HER FRAGILE BODY. SHE BROUGHT HER ARMS UP AND SCREAMED INTO MY FACE, BUT MY WEIGHT FORCED HER BELOW THE SURFACE, AND SHE CAME BACK UP COUGHING AND SPUTTERING, POUNDING MY CHEST.

I TWISTED AND SAT DOWN HARD ON HER RIGHT ARM, TRAPPING IT BESIDE HER BODY, AND HELD HER LEFT DOWN WITH BOTH HANDS AS SHE SPIT UP BRACKISH LIQUID. THE WATER WAS

CHILLY AND WHERE IT TOUCHED MY SKIN, IT COOLED MY RAGE, BUT I SAW ONLY STARS, BLACK AND BLUE BRUISES OF LIGHT FLOATING ACROSS THE SURFACE OF MY EYE, DONNIE'S FACE AS SHE CURSED AND SHOOK. THE CHILL WATER RAN CLEAR ENOUGH TO SEE THE BOTTOM, AND I PRESSED DOWN ON HER THROAT UNTIL THE BACK OF HER HEAD DENTED THE DIRT AND SAND OF THE RIVER BED.

I LOCKED EYES WITH DONNIE AND HELD HER UNDER THE WATER UNTIL SHE STOPPED BREATHING.

So that's it. That's how it ended.

What the fuck is that?

I'm looking through the newspapers for the last couple of days right now, just to see if there's some crazy story about a murder or something. Maybe I can help catch some psycho who killed a kid. Maybe there's a reward. Maybe it's all just a stupid prank. I don't know, but it's making me sick to my stomach thinking about it. When I read over what I just wrote, it makes my skin crawl.

I keep thinking about how bad I wish I'd written down whatever appeared there these last couple of days. If only I had paid more attention, but who pays attention to bathroom graffiti? Unless you're doing your business and don't have any other reading material. What am I missing? Or was it the same thing, and whoever just keeps putting it back in place when I erase it? I don't know which would be more unsettling.

— DAY 2 —

I kept a wide eye on who was hanging around the bar last night, but I can't say that it did me much good. A handful of regulars weighed down tables most of the night, wandering back and forth between the bar, the dart boards and the jukebox in the corner. The thing that's driving me crazy is, I can't see any of them drawing all over my walls.

Mookie and The Commander were at the rail for a while, shooting the shit with me. Dan and Tammy were at a table for most of the night, too. It's cute, actually. Tammy's a friend of my server, Cher. Dan used to come in here by himself, but ever since Tammy started coming to visit Cher when she's working the bar, those two kids have been in here a lot together. I don't think Dan would take his eyes off Tammy long enough to fuck around in my men's room, but who knows. I asked Cher to watch the men's last night when she was on the floor.

I don't like to make her go in there unless I'm swamped. No lady should have to see what the boys do to that bathroom on a crowd night. She's got a good eye, though, and she can multitask like a goddamn octopus.

When I let her off at one in the morning, she tells me she hasn't seen anything weird.

She asks me, "What did you want me to watch for? Guys dressed as clowns? Someone juggling urinal cakes?"

She's funny, Cher.

I tell her, "I'm afraid the mop is gonna make a break for it. He seems unhappy lately."

She chuckles her way out the door with a little wave

behind her. I don't feel like I know enough to even know what to watch out for, which I guess is why I'm writing all this down in the first place. If this ends up being a book of clues later, then I've done my due diligence.

Anyway, this morning, I get here like usual, the normal time and everything. I reach into my pocket to grab the keys, and of course I can't find them. I always drop them in my right coat pocket. My house keys and everything are all on the same ring.

I'm standing out there like an idiot, patting myself down, and I pull out my wallet, just in case the keys got jammed into it somehow. Open it up, and everything is in the wrong place. You take things for granted when you see them every day, but I know for a fact that the cards are all in different slots, and I could swear that things are missing. I had photos in there too. Family and stuff. It doesn't look right, but I swear things have been shifted.

So I'm swearing up a storm wondering how the hell things came out of the plastic sleeves, or whether I gave a picture away thinking it was a business card or something stupid like that, when I realize my keys are dangling from the index finger of my left hand.

What the hell.

First thing I do on getting inside is I check the bathroom. Can't help myself. The usual is there, naturally. An old one, right above the center toilet, so familiar now it's like an old friend. It was carved with a key. It's not going anywhere:

Please flush twice; it's a long way to the kitchen.

That appeared, I remember, around the time we tried doing some limited food service. Tacos and pub fries and stuff. They'd been pretty good, but people have to be assholes. Now it's all snacks that come in bags. You want to

21

complain about your food? Call Frito-Lay and Little Debbie, see if they give a shit.

What do you know? More weird words on the stall door, inked fresh, but not so fresh that they wipe off easy. So, here's my record of what was there before I go wipe it all off again, which I plan to do right after I snap a pic and jot it all down here:

SHE WAS STILL. HER SILENCE SCREAMED FROM DOWN UNDER. I ROLLED ACROSS THE PEBBLES, BREAKING THE SURFACE TENSION OVER AND OVER, A GEAR INTERLOCKED WITH LIVING AND TURNING AGAINST THE CONVEYOR BELT UNDERTOW.

A SHADOWY IMPRESSION GREW BENEATH ME AS I FOCUSED ON MY BREATHING, A BOY-SHAPED DENT FILLED WITH RIVER MOISTURE. SITTING THERE IN THE

FADING SUNLIGHT ON THE BANK WAS STRANGELY CALMING, THOUGH MY PULSE CONTINUED TO RACE. THE BODY HAD CEASED TO CONVEY THE MEANING OF HER, NOW AN EMPTY MEAT VESSEL NO MORE DONNIE THAN ANY OTHER SOAKED PIECE OF ROTTING DRIFTWOOD CRUMBLING UNDER THE WEIGHT OF THE RIVER'S PULL. WHAT HAD FORMERLY INHABITED THIS SHELL, THIS BELOVED ENTITY WAS NO LONGER INFUSED WITH THE SEMANTICS OF MEANING NOR ONTOLOGICAL SIGNIFICANCE. I WATCHED THE CURRENT PULL AT A GLACIAL PACE UNTIL HER SMALL, FRAGILE FORM SLIPPED DOWN TO

THE DARKER MIDDLE WHERE
THE COLORS SWIRLED, AND
HER FEATURES WERE NO
LONGER STARING THROUGH
ME.

THE WIND IN THE TREES
SOUNDED LIKE CRYING.
I STARED DOWN AT MY
HANDS. THEY HAD BECOME
ALIEN, THE FINGERS
CLAWED AND RECKLESSLY
SEARCHING LIKE TENDRILS
FOR SOMETHING TO DIGEST.
NIGHT CAME ON SUDDENLY.
JUMPING FORWARD THROUGH
TIME THIS WAY PROVED I'D
BEEN NUMB FOR HOURS, NOT
MERELY THE SECONDS THAT
HAD SEEMED TO PASS, AND I
STOOD, CHILLED TO THE BONE.

TREES TOOK ON THE QUALITIES OF AN OTHERWORLDLY BLANKET, MARRING AND SKEWING THE FADING TWILIGHT. THE FOREST TRANSFORMED AT NIGHT. THERE WAS NOTHING TO FEAR IN THESE WOODS BEYOND MY OWN WRETCHED CREATURE LIVING UNDER THIS HUMAN SKIN. I HAD BECOME A MONSTER. THERE WAS NO REASON TO RUN, NOTHING TO FLEE FROM, BECAUSE I COULDN T RUN FROM MYSELF NO MATTER HOW FAR I PUSHED MYSELF.

BRANCHES SCRATCHED, OPENING TINY ITCHY CUTS ON MY BARE ARMS. VINES AND WEEDS THREATENED TO ENSNARE ME AND BRING

ME DOWN TO THE DIRT. A BIRD SCREAMED FROM ABOVE. IT MAY HAVE BEEN A CROW, LAUGHING AT ME. BIRDS HAVE ALWAYS BEEN ASSOCIATED WITH PSYCHOPOMPS, AND THE ECHO OF ITS CALL GRABBED HOLD OF MY SQUIRMING GUTS AND PULLED ME EARTHWARD.

I RAN AND RAN UNTIL I COULDN'T SEE WHERE I WAS GOING. THE TEARS AND THE DARKNESS SWIRLED TOGETHER TO EFFECTIVELY BLIND ME. THERE WAS A NOISE IN FRONT OF ME. SOMEONE WAS THERE. I DON'T KNOW HOW I KNEW IT, BUT SOMEONE WAS STANDING THERE. I COULD FEEL A PRESENCE,

SOMETHING SOLID, BUT BREATHING, WATCHING, NOT SAYING ANYTHING.

THE TENSION BUILT INSIDE THE MARROW OF MY BONES, DOWN TO THE DEEPEST REACHES OF MY ANIMAL ANCESTRY. PREY. PREDATOR. A LAMB BEING STALKED BY A WOLF. THE SHAPE WAS BLACK AGAINST BLACK, ONLY THE FAINTEST DIFFERENCE IN INTENSITY SEPARATING THE BORDERS OF WHATEVER WAS FACING ME FROM THE SHEER NOTHING OF THE NIGHT. THE MYSTERY AND I WATCHED EACH OTHER WITHOUT SEEING.

I COULD FEEL HIM WATCHING
ME. IT WAS REALLY CREEPY.
THE DARKNESS WAS SCARY.
THEN, HE TOUCHED MY DICK.
IT WAS A BIG DICK AND HE
SAID I WANT TO SUCK
YOUR DICK FAGOT. THATS
WHY THIS STAL NEEDS A
GLORY HOLE.

For a second, that last little bit confuses me, then it clicks. I've been sitting here getting pissed off and going over that last piece again and again for about an hour now and getting more and more angry every time I read it. See, right after I'd finished writing it all down above, I'd scratched at the word "GLORY" with my nail, and it had smeared.

Just a gel pen.

Different handwriting too. Although it's hard to tell with the chicken scratch that amounts to graffiti in a bathroom stall. Still as black as the other stuff, the creepy, poetic shit, but a different kind of ink from what came before, and that's when I realize that now I've got more than one of these assholes messing with me. Tonight, when the regular crew stops in, I plan to confront them about it. Oh man, I'm pissed. I'm even taking down the "specials" board. Just watch one of those assholes ask me about what's on sale. Passive aggressive? Maybe. I have a right to be righteously raging though.

Tonight, when my regulars arrive, I will get to the bottom of this.

I am boiling. Fucking livid. I think the only thing that's keeping me from going off sideways is that I'm concentrating on being rational about this. Someone can use a pen, they can use a cleaning cloth. I just need to find out who gets to spend their weekend scrubbing my latrines.

— DAY 2 —
— LATE AFTER CLOSE —

Tonight didn't go as well as I'd hoped. We had a few strangers in. Looked like a little bachelorette party. I guess they were bar hopping. Six of them, loud and funny, buying shots with cute names. I had to sneak more than a few glances at my recipe books under the counter when they asked for "Blowjobs" and "Slippery Nipples," but it actually made me crack a smile and put me in a better mood. Having a bunch of sexy young ladies coming up over and over again to talk dirty over sweet liquor tends to make me giggle, I guess.

It was just after the girls had swaggered their way in the door that Mookie goes off to take a piss. I'm wiping down the table for the ladies, putting down a bunch of water glasses, trying to be a good host. They're thanking me and taking selfies with me; it's actually kind of fun. I hear Mookie's voice cut through the air like a thrown dagger, right in between my shoulder blades.

"Someone did a number on your stall there. Looks like a whole novel."

I probably could have held it in, maybe tamped it down like a musket ball and just kept the powder wet. But there was a round of giggles. I'm sure they didn't mean anything by it. Probably thought they were laughing with me, not at me, but hell if that didn't spark it up. I spin around and storm over to Mookie like a maniac, demanding to know what's so funny.

Mookie looks real surprised, like I just caught him naked with his hand in my cash drawer or something. He backs up a step and kind of scratches himself. "I'm just saying, Shakespeare's writing a whole new work on your bathroom walls. Crazy, man."

"There's two different styles of handwriting there. So it ain't just some poet livening up the place. You guys are fucking with me. I wanna know who's been writing all over the stall. Speak up now and maybe I won't add the cleaning bill to your tab."

Tammy asks "What, there's someone writing in the men's room?"

Dan looks over at her and he says "Yeah, there's a ton of it. It covers the whole door."

"You've seen it too?" I ask, stomping over to his table. "Working on a rough draft, college kid? Is that you?"

He looks at me like I just sprouted another head and it screamed at him. "Come on, George. I'd be proud of my work, and that doesn't even have a title."

I realize that everyone's looking at me a little off. I swallow real hard and I walk back around the bar. "Sorry. Sorry, I'm just in a foul mood. It's fine."

So now it's become a whole thing.

These girls are laughing and start asking if they can go into the men's' room to see it. "Please, come on, we're not perverts," they're saying.

Mookie of course, he's become the center of attention now, of a bunch of college girls, so he's going on and on about it, making stupid jokes about how it's practically the great American novel, only it's scatological, and the like.

"I think we should call it, *For Whom the Smell Tolls.*"

Laughs.

"Maybe *The Grunts of Wrath*?"

More.

"I was gonna' label it the *Sound and the Fury*, but apparently that one's been taken."

Now everyone is curious, and they start this mass exodus to the restroom. I keep trying to rise above the rabble, trying to tell them it's not worth it, that it's stupid. Hell, I even brought up the fire code. You really can only have like, six people in that bathroom at a time, technically.

There's a crowd of people in the bathroom. It's ridiculous. Someone starts taking selfies with their phone. It's like those people years ago who stuffed themselves into phone booths or something, only it smells like piss and bleach. Bunch of nuts. I can't even fit in through the crowd to break it up. I go back to cleaning glasses and wait for the bullshit to die down.

So a couple of minutes later, everyone files out, and now it's a party. They order more rounds right away. I can't complain. The money is coming fast and furious now, with everyone getting silly. All because of some stupid graffiti in my shitter.

As soon as things are settled, and Cher is handling the drunks, I slip into the bathroom myself to check up on things. It's pretty tidy, actually. I'm surprised that they didn't wreck the place. I unlock the center stall's toilet paper roll holder and replace the empty cardboard tube, and as I do, I force myself not to look at the door. I know it's there. I don't have to think about it right now. I don't have time. Instead, I concentrate on the roll, and notice a penciled scrawl on the holder with an arrow pointing up at the tissue:

PULL DOWN FOR ARTS DEGREE

Ouch. Ain't that the truth.

On the way out the door, I see someone has left me a new one, written right above the door handle in what appears to be blue marker.

George Patroklos Memorial Writing Center

"We're closing up. Last call!" I'm yelling as I come out the door.

Cher looks at me like I've lost my mind. I hear people "awww" and "booo" and grumble, as I storm behind the counter.

Cher asks me if I'm okay.

"Mister Patroklos, did something upset you?"

She never calls me that. It's always "George." She can tell that something is very wrong now. Her nervousness makes me even madder. Now I'm pissed that I'm pissed, which is one of the worst possible mental states to find yourself in.

"I'm fine. We're closing up. Go ahead and run the mop water. I'll finish up front."

People start charging the bar, asking what's the matter and jockeying for position for one more quick drink.

One of the young girls yells, "shots!"

I change my mind. I ask Cher to take over the front. "Never mind," I tell her. I head straight to the back and start cleaning, angrily, pacing back and forth, so hot I feel like I'm about to explode.

I know, now, hours later, they'd been trying to be funny. They'd thought they were in on the joke. Thing is, it's not a joke. I have closing chores to do now. I'm not splitting tips tonight. Cher gets all of it for putting up with my tantrums and also probably keeping me from drowning someone in their pint glass.

— DAY 3 —

Closing time took longer than I hoped. I sent Cher home, after she cleared the bar. Working in the silence helped a little bit. Just me and my thoughts. Finally, when I was done with all the necessary evils, it was time to do my due diligence.

If I'm going to document this for legal purposes, I can't stop now, no matter how pissed I am.

As expected, the real continuation from yesterday's spiraling rant is up there, sure enough, written right over the old additional words about cocksucking like those weren't even there. I guess they didn't matter much to our water closet Shakespeare. I can't leave tonight without taking a look, and just do it in the morning. No way. I guess I'm obsessed. That's what they'll say on one of those daytime TV talk shows. Whatever. The story changed. I'm documenting every damn word.

I WAITED FOR SOMETHING TO TOUCH ME, A TWIG TO SNAP, TO FEEL THE BLADE OF A KNIFE RAMMED INTO MY STERNUM, ANYTHING. BUT IT WAS JUST A LONG, SILENT

STAND-OFF, APROPOS OF NOTHING. THE LONGER I STARED THOUGH, THE MORE THE EDGES CAME INTO FOCUS, LIKE LOOKING AT A DRAWING UNDERWATER. SOMETHING TALL AND BENT IN HALF, DRAPED IN A LONG PIECE OF FABRIC, MAYBE A COAT. MOVEMENT WAS SUBTLE, LIKE AN EARTHQUAKE FELT FROM VERY FAR AWAY.

IT LOOMED OVER ME, A TOWER OF FLESH, STANDING JUST WITHIN RANGE TO LUNGE IF I RAN. I CONSIDERED MY OPTIONS. I COULD TRY TO RUSH THE FIGURE, BUT IT MIGHT BE AN ADULT, SOMEONE STRONG, PERHAPS

EVEN WITH A KNIFE OR A GUN. I COULD TURN TAIL AND FLEE INTO THE WOODS, IN THE HOPES THAT THIS GARGANTUAN BEANPOLE OF TERROR WOULD BE UNABLE TO FOLLOW ME AT SPEED, AND I COULD LOSE HIM OR HER IN THE FOLIAGE AND MAKE A BREAK FOR HOME WHEN I KNEW I WAS OUT OF REACH.

THE WORRISOME WRIGGLE IN MY GUT DID ITS BEST TO CONVINCE ME TO SCREAM FOR HELP, BUT THE RATIONAL PART OF MY MIND SILENCED THIS VOICE WITH IMAGES OF EVISCERATION, OF BEING LEFT FOR COYOTES AND INSECTS AND BIRDS TO PICK

OVER UNTIL THE POLICE FOUND MY DECAYING BODY HERE.

THE POLICE. VISIONS OF DONNIE INVADED MY SKULL, AND I WINCED FROM THE GROWING PRESSURE BETWEEN MY EARS. THERE WAS A STEADY WHINE IN MY SKULL, LIKE A FORK BEING SCRAPED ACROSS A PLATE. MY ARMS WERE GOOSEFLESH. HER EYES OPENED UP AND STARED AT ME AGAIN, LIKE SHE WAS FLOATING RIGHT IN FRONT OF ME IN THE BLACKNESS. I COULD ALMOST SEE THE MOISTURE GLEAM IN THE NEXT TO NOTHING SHINE OF

A MOONLESS CHASM ABOVE US, BUT THEN A JARRING SNAP BROUGHT ME BACK TO THE REALITY AROUND ME. THE MUSCLES IN MY CHEST CONTRACTED WITH A HISS, MY HEART ABOUT TO EXPLODE, RAZORS IN MY LUNGS.

WAS THE THING CLOSER NOW? WAS IT JUST ANOTHER TREE, OR HAD IT STALKED WITHIN STRIKING DISTANCE? SOMETHING ABOUT THE FIGURE WAS TRIGGERING RECOGNITION, EVEN THOUGH THE MISTY FORM HELD NO DISCERNABLE DETAIL. IN THE BLACKNESS, TWO CHILDREN STOOD, ONE ON THE OTHER'S SHOULDERS, TRYING TO

APPEAR MUCH LARGER THAN THEY ACTUALLY WERE. IT WAS A GAME, SOMETHING PLAYFUL, LIKE SOMETHING DONNIE AND I WOULD HAVE DONE ON A RAINY DAY INSIDE OUR MOTHER'S BOUDOIR. THERE WAS NO SOUND, NO MOVEMENT, BUT I HEARD THE GIGGLES, I SAW THEM BEND IN HALF WHERE THE TWO OF THEM SEPARATED AND THE DARKNESS FOLDED OVER UPON ITSELF. IT WAS AN UNNATURAL THING. AN ARCH WHERE PREVIOUSLY THERE WAS A BENDING ROD. AGAIN, I COULD NOT SEE ANYTHING MOVING, BUT SOME PART OF ME KNEW IT WAS HAPPENING. LIKE HYPNOSIS, WHEN A MAGICIAN TELLS HIS

VICTIM THAT THE WEATHER HAS GOTTEN COLD AND THEY ARE FREEZING. THE BODY LOWERS ITS TEMPERATURE, EVEN THOUGH NOTHING ABOUT THE AIR HAS CHANGED.

I WONDERED IF I'D GONE CRAZY. SHOULD I GO BACK TO DONNIE? SHOULD I FIND HER? WHAT WOULD I TELL MY PARENTS, THE POLICE, THE WORLD OUTSIDE THE WOODS, WHEN I RETURNED HOME WITHOUT MY SISTER, AND WITH THE BLOOD BURNING IN MY VEINS?

This has gotten me thinking about a lot of things, and I might have figured out why it's bothering me so much. That name, Donnie. Donnie is the name of my sister, who lives in Cleveland and is fine... at least... I think she's fine. Maybe I should call her? What would I say, that I read about her drowning on a bathroom wall and I figure I'd better call just in case?

When I was a kid, I used to have these vivid and terrible dreams. Not your typical stuff that scares kids, monsters and strangers and whatever, just these really image heavy, unsettling kinds of things.

I remember one where I was in some kind of hallway that was part of a factory. The edges of everything, the doors, the walls, all of it was a neon glowing blue, like electricity out of an old video game.

There was a track above me, running down the center of the hallway, and every few feet there was a huge hook, like off a crane. I was running down this hallway and looking into the doors felt like a bad idea. But eventually, I couldn't help myself, and I peered into a door on my left, and there was a mad scientist in there, like in a lab, and he has a corpse upright against a slab.

Frankenstein's monster I supposed? Maybe something I saw in a cartoon? But the setting, the filth, and these hooks, running along this track, moving toward the door at the end of the hallway, that was what I keep focusing on. There was something about that door at the end of the hall. I knew that if I saw what was in there, it would be worse than any other door in this hall, so as I came to the end of the hallway where the track headed through a black, opened doorway, I instead ducked through the door on my right.

It's a series of hallways, like a four-sided square with a block in the middle. I saw someone that looked just like me duck around the corner, and my heart leaped into my throat, and I had to chase him down. I ducked around the corner after him, but again, he was already rounding the other corner. I just saw the back of him, his long overcoat, so I ran and whipped around another corner. I wasn't gaining on him at all, and I kept catching just the smallest glimpse. There was a humming sound in the air, some kind of subsonic weight that I could barely hear, but I could feel it, and it was getting more insistent as I chased this version of myself around in circles.

I rounded a corner, feeling the sick caress of panic, and suddenly, right there in my face, was my own face looking back at me, only all the features were just dark voids. This face, it grinned at me, and all the teeth fell out, so the mouth matched the empty eyes and sallow cheeks.

He whispered, "I'm going to kill you and your sister and your mom and your dad," and then there was a gloved hand in my face and everything went dark and I screamed...

If you had ever asked me at that age to sleep with my parents, I'd have side-eyed you into next week. I was not a toddler, I was a growing boy, and yet, I was so terrified I was trembling, and I couldn't stop. My heart almost hurt, it was beating so loud and so hard. I wasn't sure what to do. I guess I was crying in my sleep, because the next thing I knew, I felt a presence in the room, and for one brief moment, I knew I was going to die. I remembered fighting every liquid in my body back, as my bladder threatened to let go, my pores began to sweat cold and my heart threatened to burst my blood vessels and let me spray a wide act of arterial fear throughout my bedroom.

"It's okay. You had a bad dream."

That was Donnie. She'd heard me tossing and whimpering and she'd come to check on me. My sister who I was supposed to protect and care for, like an avenging angel had come to rescue me. And I had to touch her arm. Only the touch of her skin would tell me that she was real. That the dream doppelganger hadn't hung her up in the kitchen, like a butchered pig, for me to find at breakfast. Dreams can be entirely too real, and the logic that defends us in our waking worlds loses power in the realm of our sleeping imagination.

This, now, is the adult equivalent of needing to touch her to see if she's really okay. This graffiti is starting to invade my dreams. Why the hell did they have to use the name Donnie, of all things?

Or, am I insane? Could be, I guess. Long hours. Tired. I really ought to call her soon.

— DAY 4 —

Quiet night at the bar, like most week-nights. The Commander is in again, talking about some crazy thing, and I usually just listen when it comes to that guy. Tonight though, I had the dumb idea to mention the bathroom ink. I figure he's an old veteran, he spends most of his time firmly planted on the bar stool. Usually takes a quick piss before he takes off for the night, but I sincerely doubt that's enough time to write a whole novel about crazy people in my stall.

Lord, he goes off when I tell him. I assure him I'm not blaming him, not after last night's mess, but something I say must have lit off a string of firecrackers behind those shining gray eyes of his. Flashbacks or some other thing, PTSD, I don't know. But as he starts off, all this crazy coming out of his mouth, I figure maybe I don't know the Commander as well as I think I do, and maybe he goes into some fugue state or something, like a sleepwalker. Maybe whatever he did in the war comes back as poetry.

Maybe there will be a match in the way he talks and the way he writes, or something. Maybe I'm just chasing ghosts. I wrote down every word, as best I could, right here:

I remember my unit was caged up in some shithole down south. We'd been told to stay put for the longest time. Might think that being in danger of catching a bullet wouldn't become just the everyday, but boredom set in long before any enemy combatants found their way down to where we were. They had sent us into combat before, those sons-of-bitches. Working our way around IEDs and patrolling dangerous areas where you were just as likely to get blown up by the old lady walking down the village square as you were getting shot by a soldier. But we'd been pulled back, set up to guard this little village back in the safe zone. Hearts and minds. Maybe. All I knew was, there was nothing to do except bake in the heat and walk around like we knew what we were doing.

And you know I seen some shit, man. Some real storms of fire. After all that action, this sitting on our asses was a god damn death sentence. I put a lot of time in with the locals, trying to kill the boredom, and believe me, there were some crazy ways to kill it dead. Even beyond the usual prostitution and drugs and gambling, there was always something to look at, something to listen to, some kind of crazy person just so vastly different than the kind of insanity you'd ever come across here in the states.

Me and my buddy Rick liked to hang out in the marketplace. The activity, I guess, was appealing, with all the stasis back at camp. There was kinetic energy to be absorbed there, felt like being a bumper in a pinball machine with the lights and sounds and metal flying around you.

One day we came across this big Arab, he was sitting there with a blanket and some cheap electronics, trinkets, some pottery, just basic stuff. He was the middle east version of a dollar store. This dude though, huge, just a giant. And almost every inch of his body was covered in tattoos. This guy had crazy ink. He was a damn fine English speaker, and we ended up shooting the shit with him for a while. Rick and I showed him our ink and asked him about his.

Some of these designs, man, it was crazy. Intricate, detailed stuff, all these symbols and sayings in Farsi between these elaborate floral patterns, animals, this whole ecosystem splashed across his body like a living mural of flesh and bone. He seemed hesitant to talk about the specifics. I mentioned the color, you know? They were vivid, like they'd been painted on and covered with shellac. It wasn't until I handed over my flask that he really started to open up. After a couple of swigs from what we liked to call the "duty free" bottle, he was all ready to talk about his ink.

He said there was this guy who lived in

a ramshackle hut on the other end of town, and this dude tattooed people old style. Needles made from bone and natural inks and techniques that most modern places would shit bricks over until they were shut down. But he said that's why everything looked so fresh and bright.

One thing I learned over there was the barter system had its benefits. A little more hooch and some coin, and our friend was convinced to play tour guide. We ended up in this dark neighborhood, barking dogs and suspicious eyes, and a dry taste of salt in the air. Our pal showed us to this shack and this skinny little dude opened a tin door bolted onto the side of what could only loosely be called a house to answer it. When he saw me and Rick, he hit the ceiling, started screaming at our friend in Farsi. Rick could speak the lingo way better than I could, so he starts saying something in a loud clear voice, repeating it over and over. I think it was either "peace be with you" or "we come in business." Something like that.

An hour later, we're sitting there inside this dude's dungeon. Rick was in an old barber chair. You know, the kind where they step down on the metal bar and your ass goes up or down? I don't remember how we got to this point. We didn't drink when we were on duty, obviously, but when you're sent to die in the desert and you get a reprieve, you start to think you're invincible, so you figure what's the worst that can happen?

Rick was telling this guy he wanted a new tattoo. I was looking at this dude's equipment, and there were no safety standards here. It wasn't like the Department of Public Health was going to come barging in and arrest this guy for not having sterile needles and plastic gloves. But it seemed clean enough, and evidence of this man's work was all over the place. There were a lot of Polaroids hung around the wall that showed what he could do. Rick was excited and ranting about putting something amazing on his bicep. A wasp or a hornet, I think, was the plan.

The artist started working, and I saw Rick's face go white. He didn't cry out, didn't scream or even whimper, but I could tell it hurt. As he was working, this dude talked about his ink. There were traps out there in the desert in the smaller villages that set up pits to trap unsuspecting invaders. Same techniques that have been used for generations out here. It wasn't just the pits though. A pit, you can climb out of, right? They'd put sharpened stakes at the bottom of these things, underneath the sand.

I asked if they were like Punji Sticks, like they had back in Vietnam. The oldest vets had stories about those. They would dig pits in the jungle, and when a soldier would fall in, the stabbing was only the beginning. The enemy would coat them with shit and poison, let them scratch you and infect your body, turn you into a dying man without having to work for it. I rambled on about this, and the skinny Arab nodded solemnly and said the Farsi word for "yes." It was different here, though, he said. Poisons and chemicals were too modern and expensive. Shit dried out here, and the bacteria wouldn't stay dangerous long enough to be a real threat. That, and the stakes didn't stab deep, because the sand didn't hold them upright like dirt would. No, these were more like needles, he told us. Like his tattoo needles, actually.

I made some stupid joke about how you could get a free tattoo that way if they'd just coat them with ink. That was when Rick yelled. A trickle of blood dribbled down his arm. The artist apologized, while our tattooed guide chuckled softly to himself.

"Exactly that," the artist said, with his eyes flashing. He dabbed up the blood on Rick's arm while clucking his tongue.

49

"This ink is the same they use to bait the traps, my friends. This ink, she gets into your blood and things change."

I asked what he meant, you know?

He said whatever story you tell with the ink, it took on the truth and could change the reality we lived in.

I was thinking, of course, this was all hill people religious bullshit or something.

But he wasn't laughing. He was dead serious. "Whatever story you write, whatever picture you paint, your art becomes concrete and your dreams manifest as truth. It is powerful, and it is dangerous."

This was sounding like some backwoods crazy tribal horseshit, but I couldn't help but feel the hair on my neck stand at attention.

Rick though, he wasn't going to show any weakness in front of me, or especially not in front of this nutcase with the needles, so he laughed this quick, forced bark and said, "Maybe I'll get hornet powers, be a superhero."

I chuckle at this of course, but this inker didn't move a single facial muscle. He just concentrated harder.

"A symbol of violence. I think, a dangerous choice, for some."

Rick laughed again, but this time it sounded more like a choke. It sounded rude.

The artist squinted a little.

"We're not here to make friends, we're here to shoot the bad guys."

I expected an "of course" or some other non-committal grunt, but there was just silence. It was contagious, and I ended up staring at the walls while they continued the scarification process.

Two hours later, it was all done, and we were looking at it in the dim light and it looked amazing. The hornet on his arm looked like it was about to fly off and away. The stinger looked sharper the combat knives we carry.

Rick paid this guy and threw in a few extra American dollars for a tip, trying to be pleasant I guess, but he was asking about after care and the guy keeps insisting it would be just fine without creams or lotions or oils or anything, and I could tell Rick was getting pissed, so I hit him on the shoulder and told him to hurry up, it was getting late.

This was not the place to be an American after dark, but we made our way back home without any trouble. We were back just in time, too. Any later and we'd have been in some serious shit. Timetables were not something to fuck with when you're enlisted. Rick, of course, was immediately showing off his ink to whoever was awake and around, and I had to admit, it looked damn fine. That tattoo was full of life and action and violence. The color was so vivid it practically shined, past the blood and smudges of discarded ink refuse streaked across his arm. He went to wash up and we heard him muffle a scream. You didn't mess with ink from a bone needle, and I remembered us thinking it was pretty funny.

Rick comes out of the washup all red faced. "It's a little sensitive."

Anyway, I remembered this pretty well because it was a turning point. More things changed than the color of his bicep. Rick started getting paranoid after that, which I never saw coming. Sure, he was full of bravado, but he was a good guy, you know? But he started flying off the handle real easy, grumbling about the civilians, things like that.

Two weeks later, I found him.

Patrol. Me and another guy, Dan, we were out patrolling the perimeter of our camp, and there was this lump in the road. I saw it first.

"Hold up," I said.

Dan stopped, and I saw his hand go toward his firearm. Nothing about this looked right.

We had to be real careful most of the time.

This was not a straightforward kind of fight. The bombs weren't big, round black balls with comic book fuses. Might be a shopping cart full of rugs, or a mound of shit, or a woman out walking, you didn't know until shit went down, so everything was worth checking out before you stumbled over it.

This was just a heap, and as we came a little closer, I saw it was a body. It was impossible to tell what the situation was at a glance. It was shrouded in some kind of loose cloth, which was blowing in the desert wind, shredded like an ancient relic.

Dan crept up closer and took a look, and the next thing I knew he was frantically waving me over.

I'm just about to ask if we need to call a disposal unit when I saw the green uniform underneath the cloth.

Rick was barely a man, he was so swollen. Like a tick filled with blood, a meat balloon, peach, pink, red and white all scrambled together in a garbled mess of skin. There were hundreds of tiny red sores bloating up like infection all over his exposed skin. His eyes were swollen shut and purple hued, his tongue so thick it was forced out between his bruised lips.

Dan called the medics while I quietly threw up on the side of the road.

It hurt a lot. One of my best friends. That's bad enough, definitely the kind of thing that haunts you, but sometimes things are even worse than the death of a friend. The circumstances around it, those are the things I still have nightmares about sometimes.

I had to know, so I asked around, tried to stay on top of the news and figure out what had happened to my friend. They quarantined the body at first. Anyone would have, seeing it like that. It could have been any number of diseases or plagues, something new and unseen, some rare version of shingles, so those first few days were terrifying. A sense of anxiety hung all over camp, with rumors flying about some deadly new desert disease that made your skin erupt.

I was involved with filing the reports, since I'd been one of the guys who'd found Rick, and I had some friends in the medical tent, and well, the official cause of death was massive poisoning by any number of stings and bites. He'd been completely overloaded with deadly stinging wounds from some kind of creature. We had seen the occasional scorpion out there. Some spiders and flies. But this had been a swarm.

"Like wasps or hornets," the doctor told me.

Gallows humor. I couldn't help but

chuckle. "Like his tattoo."

"Tattoo?"

I told the doc about his brand-new ink. "Didn't you see it?"

The doc told me he hadn't seen a tattoo. That arm was blank skin. Nothing there but the marks of a hundred poisoned daggers no bigger than the end of a push pin.

So I have to wonder, now. Where did that hornet go?

After that, The Commander clams up again. Some guy nearby offers to buy him a drink, and he takes up the offer, orders a whiskey, neat. He deserves it. It had been spellbinding. The way he'd told me the story, I have to admit, it was spooky. Got quiet after that, just nursing his drink.

So, here's the thing. The Commander has been coming in here for years, and he's talked to me plenty about his time in the military. He's told me several times over the years that during the war he was actually stationed a few thousand miles away, over in Asia. Japan or Korea I think. Nowhere near the fighting. He was a maintenance guy, took care of vehicles. He'd repaired engines. Everything from painting to fixing the machines.

We don't call him the Commander because of some crazy war experience, or like he led some kind of Sergeant Fury's Howling Commandos. It was a fun nickname, because he always used to come in with his old military patches and whatnot from his time in the service. This had been the story for years, and it had been told in an offhand way that didn't stretch the concept of truth at all.

Here's what's weird: I have a lot of experience reading people. Somewhere around half my clientele I get in here come in to talk to someone. It's a less expensive form of therapy and the drugs are way cheaper. I'm listening to this story and scanning his facial features for a tic, listening for a catch in his voice, or even the overconfidence that comes from believing your own lies. Some people tell stories with religious zeal, and they have become infected with their own viral bullshit, which is a dangerous kind of storyteller.

The Commander was absolutely one hundred percent telling the truth.

Either that, or he's the greatest poker player alive and I should close this place up and take him to Vegas. I haven't been able to stop thinking about this all night. My brain knows better, based on the information I've stored up from past conversations and memories. This man never saw a bullet fired, never disarmed a bomb, hell, probably hasn't even been in the desert. My heart, my instinct, my gut, they tell a different story about this casual conversation, one that makes it impossible to find a resolution between the various parts of me.

Can something be both true and false at the same time? If two concepts completely contradict each other, how can they both be true? It's like two mutually exclusive ideas somehow overlap and end up taking up the same space.

Specific gravity tricks are in a bartender's repertoire, things that show a concrete separation and can be backed up by physics and the properties of matter.

Sticking with the military theme, the thing that sent my brain spiraling down this road, here's how to make a B-52:

- One part Grand-Marnier.

- One part Bailey's.

- One part Kahlua.

Just like with events, the order of operations matters. Did you add the Kahlua first, or the Grand-Marnier? Did I stay close to family, or did I feel like I had nobody to stay at home for and moving away was a better choice? Did the Commander learn to shoot a rifle and go off to war or enlist as a mechanic? The Grand-Marnier has a specific gravity of 1.03. The Kahlua's is 1.16. The Bailey's, somewhere in between at 1.05. If you started with the lightest one, the heaviest is going to slam into it and cut right through, instead of creating those beautiful, perfect layers. What if you used Brandy instead of Grand-Mariner? Then it would cut through the Bailey's. Your perfect layers would be destroyed. The whole drink would not only taste different, but it would appear different, and the spell would be broken, the effect, ruined. So what about those choices we make? How do they manifest themselves? Then, even if we make all the right choices, what happens if a muddler penetrates the surface of our perfect mix and breaks the tension? How does our certainty transform into something alien and frightening?

This isn't that. If it isn't that, what is it?

— DAY 5 —

It's silent. A quiet beyond silence. An isolation tank, a space so still and empty that it goes past any silence you've ever heard and gets noisy again. Even in the country, late at night, in the middle of a family farm, out under the stars, in the pitch blackness of endless space, you hear things.

Listen.

Crickets. Distant coyotes in the hills. Running water.

The small town still has highway traffic blazing through the endless night, just over the hill.

But in total silence, you can really focus in and you start to hear the real sounds underneath everything else, that are so quiet and so ubiquitous that you've never realize you've heard them your whole life.

Your heart beating. Your blood rushing through your ears. Every tiny crick and creak of your joints as you stretch out a limb to feel where you are, to try and find something familiar in the lightless void.

Wood. Boards. Very close. I'm lying on my back, facing up, or so my inner ear tells me. My stomach drops. A coffin. I'm underground.

No. My elbows are floating in cold space, past the barrier I imagine there, and now I'm feeling around with my fingertips. Wood under me, wood over me. Floorboards.

I listen to my own breathing, concentrating on the slow inhale and exhale. I feel lucid. If this is a dream, should I wait for the other boot to drop on my face, the false bottom to plunge me off the cliff, the monster to grab my throat, or is there really just nothing here but me?

I feel like I'm coming back into my body from an astral projection, something the scientists would call the aftermath of sleep paralysis, electric tingles lightning cracking their way through my capillaries and into my limbs. There's no light. Nothing but the sound.

Slowing my breathing. Then stopping. Holding for four.

One.

Two.

Three.

Four.

Then breathing in for another four count. And holding again.

One.

Two.

Three.

Four.

This is something called square breathing. An ex-girlfriend of mine who'd been really into yoga had taught me this trick to help alleviate stress and nerves. Each four count is a different color. Red, blue, green, yellow. One, two, three, four. Repeat as often and as long as necessary to feel better, to be more at peace, to come back into your body when something is trying to rip you out of it through the anxieties of your mind.

The secondary effect, the one I'm sure will come, is that it allows me to tune in better on my surroundings. Taking my mind off my own sounds and expanding my net to see what else I can pick up. This is animal level survival stuff, basic, primal lizard brain sensory tricks that predators and prey alike have used for eons to gain an upper hand.

Somehow, I know I will hear something.

As my breathing slows down and falls into a pattern, I begin to notice the variations coming from up above, and as I do, every hair on my body stands up.

I inhale. One. Two. Three. Four. I hold. One. Another

inhale from somewhere above me. Two. From somewhere else, an exhalation. Three. Someone else is breathing. Four. Right above the boards. We are separated by this thin layer of construction.

The smell of my laundry soap, my own linens, my body, it's everywhere. I realize with sudden terror where I lay. Somehow, I am in the crawlspace below my home. I am underneath the floor.

Someone else is in my house.

Now, my eyes begin to adjust to the light, my pupils open to gigantic black pools, grabbing desperately at every available photon in my terror, and there is just enough here. Just enough to see the outline, to know the architecture, to remember the blueprints in my floor safe and to understand the dimensions of where I am.

This is my bedroom. I am underneath my own bed. And there is someone sleeping in my bed. Right above me. Close enough to reach out and strangle.

A dream, right? So I know this is going to sound completely crazy, but I'm having actual anxiety attacks. Never in my life, before, have I had dreams like this. I keep thinking about this writing I'm doing, and there's all this uncertainty. Sleep is something that I have always taken for granted. That mysterious time when the brain derails the train of thought and allows itself to be still. My nightmares from when I was little have been moved to long term memory storage. Nothing to be missed though. Obviously, I'm making new ones.

I don't remember writing about my dreams, in any detail. I remember waking up, sweating, my heart pounding, and I remember grabbing for the headboard and slamming my finger down on the switch to the lamp, hurting my fingernail. I'd been still half asleep, groggy, confused, and I think I grabbed the book and wrote, but this morning, I can't remember the dream at all. Reading over it again just now, I feel sick. I have to change my sheets out, just to feel like everything is mine and I am safe in my own bedroom.

Maybe, if these writings become evidence in a destruction of property suit or whatever, I should tear these particular pages out. From a legal standpoint, they're not relevant to the case. But, then, I don't know what's relevant anymore.

My niece, Ellen, last time I'd visited the family, we'd had a hell of a talk. I remember she was sitting off to the side in an orange and red lawn chair on the back porch at her grandma's house. We'd all been there, kind of a family reunion thing, kind of a first time seeing our new baby thing for one of my cousins, everyone getting together for once and trying to scrape together enough common ground to stand on, while the yard shrinks all around us. So Ellen had looked bored, and I'd always gotten along real well with my sister's kids. They're good kids, bright, kind of artistic and a little weird, but I like that. A bartender has to get along with a variety of characters, or he wouldn't be able to do the job for very long.

I take my beer over and sit down, and start shooting the shit with my niece, just casually asking her about her life, school and boys and summer jobs and the like. We're both readers, her and I. She's a lot more voracious about it than I am, of course. I don't have time like I used to, to keep up with what's going on in the book world, but that kid always has a book cracked open. Eventually, the conversation heads that direction and she's telling me about what she's been reading.

Like I say, this kid is smart, and she starts telling me about this science fiction stuff she's getting into. Alternate realities, many-worlds theory, space and time and the mysteries of the universe. Many worlds. That's a thing, I guess. As she goes on, I realize she has dropped the FI and is just talking SCI, which I find unsettling. So the idea is, that every tiny thing we do, every choice we make where there are multiple possible outcomes, splits the universe into different paths. In this one, I get a cat, in that one, I get a dog. Eventually, all these little fractures lead to infinite universes where everything possible or impossible has happened or will occur.

I humor Ellen, listening intently. I used to like watching Star Trek, and the Twilight Zone, I have no problem entertaining these crazy theories. It's fun, you know? So I mostly forgot about them until recently.

I find myself thinking about The Commander's story, and I wonder about these barriers between universes. I wonder how thin those membranes are, and whether someone can stand on the edge of one. If someone is standing on the border, does he see both worlds?

What happens if he's standing there when a split happens?

I guess in infinite universes he falls into one, and in infinite other universes, he falls into the other one, but then, aren't there infinite universes too where he stands on that line?

Does he tear in half, each part of him shooting off into a dying star somewhere, plasma swallowing him up until he's nothing more than primordial matter again?

Do his mind and his body shake hands and go their separate ways?

He goes to war and kills the enemy. He paints jeeps and fucks local women. He guards the tilt-a-whirl. Maybe they're all true at once.

My head hurts.

— DAY 6—

Last night, something weird happened.

I closed up the bar and got out around two thirty. I had a couple of shots with a few of my regulars, but I make it a policy to never get tipsy at my own bar, so I was pretty careful.

That makes what happened even weirder.

Last thing I'd done was take an inventory. Things carved into the walls, inked up on the doors, scratched into the hand-dryer by the sink, everything I could find. Even stuff I've seen a million times before.

Very little in the ladies' room, but I'd been surprised to find a few nuggets of wisdom.

Black, thick sharpie:

spank me like you mean it.

Immediately under that in black pen:

but you mean nothing to me.

I always thought about converting this place into a dyke bar. Every lesbian I've ever met, I've liked. Sometimes I think I like them better than the guys who come in. They tend to clean up after themselves better, and I like flannel shirts.

Next to the sink, in carefully lettered blue pen:

Stay in drugs.

Eat your school.

Don't do vegetables.

That one, I leave up, because it's funny.

Of course someone's turned the directions on the hand dryer into instructions on how to press the button and receive bacon, but that's a pretty common joke on those machines, and it's scratched into the metal, and I don't really think that's what's bothering me about the situation. There's also a tiny drawing of a little goblin dude in one of the stalls that uses the hole where the hook used to be on the door as an eye socket. Reminds me of one of those old hotrod illustrations with the rockabilly monsters street racing with their tongues lolling out, spraying a trail of drool into the dust behind them.

The men's room, naturally, is filled with words and pictures, as for some reason my sex cannot occupy themselves with the simple pleasures of eliminating waste when in the restroom. It has to be a forum. I've mentioned the condom machine and the center toilet stall previously, but here's a list of other gems currently taking up space in the pisser:

Marker, above the left urinal:

Chicken Livers are full of vitamin P!

In the left stall, some poor young drunk, suffering through some bout of unrequited love, had written something pretty sexist and awful, but it's in permanent marker, so it may live there for a while. It says:

*Remember, no matter how much
you like her, someone somewhere
is already sick of her shit.*

On one side of the stall:

toilet tennis

Look right

On the other side:

toilet tennis

Look left

Right stall has a carving in the door:

*OPIUM IS THE RELIGION OF
THE MUSES.*

Also scratched in the paint, probably with a key:

Jesus Saves.

Written in ballpoint pen underneath, layered several times
to be legible:

at Kmart and you can too.

Of course, it's that center stall door that keeps changing
on me.

The idea of home is one we construct, walls woven from the thread of memories, boards of experience holding up walls constructed from our sense of belonging and being safe. Depending on our experiences there, home is a refuge, a charmed space, intricately etched with countless wards against threats and foes and the unfortunate ichor of real life outside its walls.

The familiar shape: a rectangular box with gabled roof, chimney thrust on top like a cherry

STEM. JAGGED FENCE ON ONE SIDE OF A SINGLE TREE ERUPTING FROM THE MIDDLE OF THE YARD, DOWN TO THE ONE SINGLE PORCH LIGHT CHASING THE SHADOWS AWAY FROM THE FRONT PORCH. INSTEAD, I COME UPON AN ALIEN MONOLITH, A HIVE, BUZZINGWITHSUPERNATURAL ENERGY, THE HEAT OF HELL COMING FROM IT IN WAVES THAT SCORCHES THE EARTH AND SALTS ITS WOUNDS.

INTHISMOMENT,INTHISPLACE, I FEEL MY BRAIN SPLIT IN TWO DIFFERENT DIRECTIONS. IN ONE WORLD, I CONFESS, CRY, SCREAM, SAY IT WAS AN ACCIDENT, TAKE THEM TO

THE PLACE WHERE IT HAD ALL HAPPENED, WHERE THE LIGHT IN HER EYES HAD GONE OUT. IN THE OTHER, A SHIFT, SPACE MOVING AROUND THE SITUATION UNTIL IT FITS A NEW SHAPE, ONE WHERE I'D LOST TRACK OF HER IN THE DARKNESS, WHERE I'D CALLED AND SEARCHED BUT FOUND NO SIGN, WHERE WE'D NEEDED THE AUTHORITIES TO SEARCH THE WOODS, TO MOUNT A MASSIVE MANHUNT FOR DONNIE. SURELY, SHE COULD HAVE BEEN STILL BE ALIVE. SURELY, NOTHING HAPPENED.

A BILLION EGGS HATCH IN THE PIT OF MY STOMACH, MAKING

ME RETCH VIOLENTLY. MY
INTESTINES TWIST INTO
MOEBIUS STRIPS OF GUILT
AND PAIN. I REACH UP AND
TOUCH THE CORNERS OF
MY EYES, DRENCHED WITH
TEARS I HADN'T KNOWN I
WAS CRYING. MY BODY IS
A WRECK, GIVING OUT ON
ME AS I RUN THE LAST FEW
FEET UP TO THE PORCH,
AND THEN STOP. I CAN GO NO
FARTHER. MY LEGS REFUSE
TO MOVE, EVEN AS MY INSIDES
CHURN VIOLENTLY IN EVERY
DIRECTION POSSIBLE.

I AM STILL STANDING OUTSIDE,
ROOTED TO THE SPOT, WHEN
MY FATHER OPENS THE FRONT
DOOR AND SEES ME, STANDING

THERE, SHIVERING, TEARS AND SNOT RUNNING DOWN MY RED AND SWOLLEN FACE. IT'S HARD TO REMEMBER WHAT HAPPENED AFTERWARD, IN THE IMMEDIATE. THERE ARE BLANKETS AND HOT DRINKS AND FRANTIC CALLS TO THE AUTHORITIES. THERE ARE INTERVIEWS AND SIRENS AND TALL MEN TRYING TO CONCEAL THEIR PANIC WHEN ASKING FOR DETAILS ABOUT WHAT I'D EXPERIENCED AND WHAT MIGHT HAVE HAPPENED TO SEPARATE MY SISTER AND I.

THE ONLY POSSIBILITIES I SEE BEFORE ME ARE CONFESSION OR OBFUSCATION OF THE TRUTH. I CAN'T STAY SILENT.

That will speak louder
than any other option.
There are no other
options. The thing had
happened. There is no
choice to live in a world
where I do not hold
Donnie under the water
until her brain ceases
all activity, until I watch
her perish under my own
hands, and I see her eyes
wide open and white like
wet soap every time I
close my own, forever.

Nobody and everybody
believes the story. Once
they find her body, there
is yet more confusion, but
nothing to suggest that

SHE HASN'T SLIPPED INTO THE STREAM AND SOMEHOW BEEN UNABLE TO GET BACK ABOVE THE SURFACE. NOTHING TO SUGGEST THAT THE PERSON SHE'D TRUSTED MORE THAN ANYONE HAD ROBBED HER OF EVERYTHING IN ONE MOMENT OF ELECTRIC MADNESS, MISTRUST AND MISFIRING SYNAPTIC PATHWAYS.

IT'S HATE THAT FEEDS US.

So I start walking home, and I get thinking about the graffiti. Ugly. In every way, I mean that. I wonder how there could be nothing there except a few scuff marks from where I've been scrubbing off the junk every morning this past week and then the very next time I look, it's back again. There's something about the blackness of that ink that makes me feel like it's permanent, but then it does come off. I consider grabbing a slice from the bodega on the corner, but I figure pizza that's been sitting under a heat lamp for four hours isn't going to do my digestive system any favors. I almost drop in there and buy one anyway, just to get my mind on something else, even if it's where to wipe the grease while I'm walking, but I don't stop. I'm humming stupid songs, trying to get an earworm going, just to annoy myself to the point where I can stop thinking about work. I don't like to take work home with me.

I read a self-help book once where they wrote all about how we go on this journey of understanding whenever we pick up a particular skill set or new information. You start with unconscious incompetence, meaning you don't know that you don't know what you're talking about. Like, I'm sure there's some kind of specialized position in a water treatment plant that involves some guy fishing human remains out of the wastewater, but I don't know what they print on his name tag, or what's on his tax forms. So then, you get a little smarter about a thing and you move on to conscious incompetence. That's when you understand that there's something you don't know about. Like, if you read a book on airplanes and you've seen all the diagrams with the parts and where they go, all of a sudden you know about what you don't know.

After that, you move on to conscious competence, which is where most people stay with most things in their lives. That's when you know what you're doing and can do the job. You've read the book, you know how to make all the cocktails and what the difference between a lager, an ale and a stout is and how they make them.

But, there's a step after that too, which most people don't think about. It's called unconscious competence, which is when you've traced the neural pathway so often in your brain that it's carved a groove there like a record. When you've walked the same path every day for years, back and forth, stopped at the same street corners, seen the same building facades and yards, the same homeless people, the same clubs closing down with the same doorman nodding at you, the same bent street signs, well, you don't need to think about where you're walking anymore. It's become a part of you.

You blank out.

Like, when you drive to work the same way every day,

after a couple of months of that, you sometimes don't re-member the last five minutes of your drive and have to wonder where your mind went, something like that.

I've walked that same couple of blocks between the bar and my apartment for years. Let's assume I've gone into work three hundred and sixty days a year, with those few vacation days or when I've been sick and had to have Cher or someone open the place up for me. I've been doing that for a decade now, give or take. I walk almost every day, except once in a while if it's real cold or raining to drown me when I'll drive over. Back and forth, that's two trips along that same route every day, only one of them in re-verse. That's something over seven thousand times. Even if my mind is fixed on something else, I still end up where I'm going at the end and blink myself awake to the world knowing right where I'm at. Maybe there's a moment of disorientation, but it's so ingrained in me, it's a part of me. It's like I'm on rails.

Somehow, last night, I ended up getting myself lost.

I don't know how it happened, but somewhere between the bodega and home, I ended up walking off on a fun-ny path. I didn't notice until some part of me above water called out to the braindead autopilot "Hey, don't you think it's awfully dark out tonight?" I shook my head, sucked down the cool night air and felt my feet drag to a stop un-derneath me.

I didn't recognize the street. Part of that was that it was so dark. Not a single streetlight was on around me, just endless black with the faintest glow coming from be-hind a few shades here and there. I turned around and looked back the way I came, but I didn't see any lights on down there either. It made me a little nervous, wandering around the street at night without knowing exactly where I was, but I figured, I could take care of myself, I was street savvy, probably just a power outage.

Sure enough, just about the time I finished that thought, I saw daggers of brilliant white light shooting out of an alley about fifty yards down the street. With a light like that, it had to be the back entrance to a club or something, or at least an emergency light. Somewhere I could stand for a minute, check my GPS and get my bearings, or clear my head and figure out where the hell I wandered off to.

It was an alley, definitely. Dumpsters. A wooden box with an old, broken padlock on it framed some electric breakers. A couple of old signs to beware of electric shock nailed up nearby. The refuse of a lot of lives lived fast in cramped quarters, typical of the city. The alley hooked off to the left down at the other end, and as I was looking around, the lamp above me blew out with a sizzle and a crack. I jumped like someone was shooting.

Now, I was starting to get nervous. I know I'm a grown man, but there was something about being out in the dark, all alone, an insignificant sack of meat and breath in the abyss, that just made the hairs on the back of my neck stand up and try to pull themselves free.

The hum and click of something powering up, and then there was another light source. This one was coming from around the corner, up ahead. I shook my head and walked up to the corner to take a look. This alley, it looked long. I could see maybe twenty feet in, where the edge of this new lamp stopped throwing its light, but after that, man, it was just dark and cold and empty.

I was walking toward the light though, prompted by that same inner lizard part that drove our caveman ancestors toward light and water and shelter. There was just some part of me that was attracted to the idea of being safe, and this light represented that. As soon as I got under it, I pulled out my phone and took a quick look around just to make sure I didn't miss some creep waiting in the dark, but no, there was nothing, just silence and the smell of the concrete jungle's filthy edge.

As soon as I pushed the button on my phone, I knew I was screwed. It beeped at me and in this faded sort of dim attempt to work, it flashed the battery warning. It was on just long enough to show me zero bars and no signal before it flipped to the phone logo and powered itself back down. Did someone detonate an EMP or something over the city? Did those even work like they do in the movies? With all the power fluctuations, I was starting to think it was some kind of terror attack or something, but who the hell would attack this neighborhood, especially at three in the morning?

The light above me cut out again, but now there was one farther up along the way, just outside the circle of light I had been standing in just moments before.

More old brickwork, some with graffiti, which for some reason really angered me.

Seeing it put me back in my head for a second, and I felt like I was in a waking dream, but I was way too lucid for that.

There was this big mural type set of letters in silver and blue and black, the kind that skater kids liked to put up when they go tagging. Instead of a set of initials or something though, it read:

The Indifference of Heaven.

I stormed up to the wall, about to kick a garbage can into it, but the light blew with an electric snap and there was yet another one up ahead of me again.

There was nowhere else to go. I had to keep moving.

I didn't know if I was getting farther away from my street, or closer, and I didn't like being all turned around, but there really wasn't any other option. I needed to find a convenience store, or something familiar to orient myself.

The next light did the same thing, popped out as soon as I got under it, but now there was a familiar yellow way up ahead in the distance. If I squinted, I saw motion, once, then once more a few seconds later, and I realized that what I was seeing must be cars. That was promising, but there was a long stretch of darkness between me and the street, and my mind flooded with visions of tripping over some crazy person with violent tendencies in the dark, falling into a damaged manhole or an old storage cellar, rat bites, used needles, all the madness that might be there waiting for me like snakes in tall grass.

Step by step, I shambled forward, testing any particularly dark patch with a quick kick from the tip of my shoe before putting my foot down. There were definitely cars up ahead. Not a lot of them, but enough to give me hope that I was about to stumble back out into a place I could find on a map. But as I was walking by where the alley took a turn, where the newest white light had turned on and hummed above like a giant fly, I turned my head to see if there was anything else down that way.

Someone was standing there, just past the edge of the light. I let out a yelp, and then composed myself, a little ashamed. There was no reason to assume that the shape I saw was anything else but another guy out for a night walk or lost in the rolling blackout that had infected this neighborhood. But then, as I was looking, he stepped into the light, and if there was another way to put this that made more sense, I would, but this character was illuminated from above. No smile, no color, just a sharp contrast seven-foot giant wobbling slightly, staring right at me, eyes nothing but shadows hidden by the brim of his hat.

My mind couldn't make sense of it, but every bit of me somehow knew, in the way you know in a dream that a place that didn't look right was still your grandma's house, or your local coffee shop, that it was two kids playing dress up in an extra-long trench coat and fedora. Like an old film noir joke. It had to be, because this tall thing was just looking at me with a smooth-as-glass baby face, bent in the middle like he was a loose top half trying to balance on his friend's shoulders. Why, then, didn't I feel safe? Why did looking at them make my stomach turn and my legs liquify into gelatin?

It shifted, and the edges moved. The outline rippled

and squirmed like liquid. Where limbs should have been, first it seemed like tentacles, then wings, then insect pins, then a hand reaching out for me with too many fingers. My brain screamed that I had to be hallucinating, because this writhing shadow demon couldn't be real; the way it moved and the unsettling feelings that rose up in my guts when I looked at it tore into me like food poisoning. I should have run, or called out, or screamed, or something, but it took everything I had in me just to remember to breathe.

I slowed my walk for a second, and as soon as I did, the pair of kids, or the man, or whatever melted back in shadow. I didn't see him take a step, but the shadow swallowed them up anyway.

Now that I couldn't see it anymore, it could be anywhere. There were a million shadows around me in every direction, and my skin crawled across my bones as I felt the electric tingle of fingers just about to touch me on every part of my body and pull me into that black nothing.

I lurched forward, gasping with panic. It took me just a few seconds to get to the other end, where the alley spit me out onto the road. I stumbled out of the mouth of the darkness and was relieved to see street lights, the distant lit up signs of diners and restaurants, and a few headlights and taillights doing their dance along the highway. It took me a second to get my bearings then, because there was no way I was near the highway. The highway was miles from my apartment and my bar.

I turned around, and what do you think I saw? Nothing. I'm on the side of the god damn highway. It was just a residential street about a hundred yards beyond the exit ramp for the expressway. There was no fucking alley. There was nothing but a couple of quiet homes, sleeping in their peaceful neighborhood, and me, standing on the side of the road just about to run up the embankment into oncoming traffic.

I hoofed it over to a convenience store and had to ask the clerk for the address to figure out where I was. Poor kid looked at me like I was on drugs. I must have looked scared out of my mind. Somehow, I'd walked over four miles. I had no business whatsoever being where I was, and there was no way I could have walked that long without my feet feeling like I'd been dancing on nails. That phrase kept going through my head on the cab ride home. *The Indifference of Heaven*. Made me wonder if heaven was watching out for that kid and his friend I saw, or whether it gave a shit about what any of us were up to at three in the morning.

— DAY 7—

I know I locked the door.

I checked the bathroom before I left.

When I got in today, the words were back. More words. New words.

It doesn't make any sense. I check with the owner of the building, and there's no night cleaning crew or anything I'm unaware of. He laughs when I ask him, in fact. Says that there's no way he was paying for overnight carpet cleaners without getting me involved. I say that's funny, because I don't even have carpets. He doesn't involve himself much other than collecting rental fees and taxes.

Then he gets a little concerned. He asks if there was a break-in, and whether I'd talked to the cops.

"No, no break-in," I tell him. "The place was still locked up tight when I got here."

"If you want to hire a security guard, we can talk about that."

Is that a solution? For a bathroom?

He asks me if something is missing.

I almost say, no, *something was left behind,* but then I shut my trap. Explaining this is going to make me sound nuts.

But the words, the words, more and more no matter what I do. Again, more evidence for the file, because these things escalate, and I'll be damned if I don't have my records in order when it's time to reconcile all debts.

IT BEGAN, AS ALWAYS, WITH THE FACE OF THE LOCUST. MY FACE WAS SEWN TOGETHER FROM SCRAPS, TWO HALVES ALIGNED TO APPEAR ONE WHOLE, BUT TEEMING WITH MICROSCOPIC LIES. IT PEELED APART AND REVEALED THE SUBTEXT IN THE MORNING MIRROR, ALIVE WITH REPULSIVE AND ENTICING QUALITIES. THIS WAS THE INFINITE TIME. I BEGAN COUNTING AT THE FIRST AND STOPPED AFTER A DOZEN. THE LOCUST WAS A HARBINGER OF SOMETHING UNKNOWN, A QUANTITY YET TO BE FIXED AND ONLY WRITTEN UNDERNEATH MY SKIN. I REMEMBERED, THAT

MORNING, STROKING MY PALE
SKIN AND LETTING A FINGER
TRAIL DOWN THE BRIDGE OF
MY NOSE, EXPECTING THE
SKIN TO ERUPT, TO SEE
WHATEVER HORRORS LAY
BENEATH, BUT MY FACE
JUST REFLECTED MY OWN
CONCERNED EXPRESSION.

BENEATH PINK LIPS AND A
JUTTING JAW LINE, THERE
WERE A MILLION MANDIBLES
READY TO DEVOUR. BURIED
UNDER EACH SOFT BROWN
EYE WAS A COMPOUND
GRIDWORK OF OPTIC NERVES
LIKE A SECURITY CAMERA
ROOM FULL OF FEEDS. I
FELT THE TOP OF MY SCALP,
KNOWING THAT THE CURLS OF

MEDIUM BROWN HAIR THERE HID THE SLITHERING ROLLS OF ANTENNAE BENEATH THE SKIN'S SURFACE. I COULD NOT FEEL THESE THINGS, BUT THE LOCUST STARED BACK AT ME, REGARDLESS.

HOW MANY TIMES HAD I AWOKEN IN THE MORNING BEFORE SCHOOL TO FEEL THAT SECOND LAYER OF PAPER-THIN SKIN JUST BENEATH MY OWN, SKIN THAT I COULDN'T REACH TO SCRATCH WHEN THE ITCHING BEGAN? I TOLD DONNIE ABOUT IT AFTER THE FOURTH TIME I SAW THE VACANCY IN MY OWN REFLECTION. SHE LAUGHED

AT ME AND HUGGED ME. SHE SAID THINGS WERE GOING TO BE FINE. I BELIEVED HER.

I STARTED TO JOT DOWN THE COINCIDENCES AND MARKED MOMENTS OF DIFFERENCE WHEN THE LOCUST APPEARED, TRYING TO FIND PATTERNS. I WAS ILL EQUIPPED. IT WAS TRYING TO FIND THE END OF A SINGLE STRAND OF SPAGHETTI IN A SERVING BOWL WITHOUT MOVING ANY NOODLES. MY INSIGHT WAS CRIPPLED, EVEN AS I TRIED TO CHECK IN WITH MYSELF AND FURTHER UNDERSTAND WHAT THE OMEN MIGHT MEAN, WHETHER IT WAS AN OMEN AT ALL,

AND HOW FAR INTO REALITY
THESE FEELINGS OF MINE
HAD PENETRATED.

BEING TURNED DOWN BY
SOMEONE I ASKED TO THE
HARVEST DANCE.

FAILING A TEST.

BEING BEATEN BY THE
STRANGE KIDS WHO LIVED
OUT IN THE WOODS.

EVEN YESTERDAY'S
INCIDENT WITH DAD.

THE LOCUST WAS PRESENT
IN ALL OF THESE.

THERE WAS NO STRATEGY
TO FOIL MY PERCEPTIONS
THAT WOULD DIMINISH THESE
FEELINGS, SO I IGNORED IT AS
BEST I COULD. THE SUMMER
WAS HOT, AND THE OUTDOORS
WAS FREEING, OPEN AND
FRESH, AND GOING THERE
SEEMED LIKE AN ADEQUATE
WAY TO SUPPRESS ANY
INVASIONS.

BUT THE WAY THAT WATER
CALLED TO ME, LIKE A FIELD OF
CORN WAITING TO BE TURNED
TO CHAFF, A LIQUID LOVER
COOLED INTO ICE. I FELT THE

SKIN ON THE BACK OF MY HANDS PRICKLE. DONNIE'S LITTLE BETRAYALS FELT LIKE HOT KNIVES THROUGH THE BUTTER OF MY INSIDES. IT WASN'T THAT SHE WOULDN'T SAY SHE WAS SORRY, OR THAT SHE WAS INCAPABLE OF UNDERSTANDING WHAT SHE HAD TRULY DONE TO ME, OR TO US, IN THESE PAST FEW WEEKS OF SUMMER. THE PART THAT FELT LIKE SWALLOWING A PILLOWCASE FULL OF SEWING NEEDLES WAS THIS: SHE WOULD NEVER UNDERSTAND HOW SHE HAD HURT ME. SHE WAS TOO SELF-INVOLVED. LIKE A METASTASIZING CANCER, HER CENTER PULSED WITH WAVES OF ROT THAT

AFFECTED THE CELLS AROUNDHER, ANDIWASSIMPLY ANOTHER CELL. I WISHED I'D NEVER SWALLOWED THOSE PILLS. I WISHED I'D TOLD HER NOTHING. I WISHED I WAS SOMEONE ELSE. THE LOCUST BUZZED.

It's ultimately just graffiti, not a federal offense. Not a felony. Unless, like I said, this is a confession of someone's crimes. But, I don't think so. This is too out there. Reads like some Twilight Zone Ray Bradbury shit, not like letters in the paper from the Zodiac killer. All I know is that I'm not comfortable here anymore. That's an alien feeling for sure. This is my home away from home. It's mine. Where my chosen family spends their time. Where I willfully spend my time and energy and heart, and... I don't know.

I keep track and stay sharp.

If it's one of my regulars, I swear I'll kill them.

I don't like those thoughts, but they're coming hot and fast.

I talked to the cops, and I emailed my alderman. They pretty much had the same reply. The cops cited the destruction of property laws and asked the value of the bathroom stall. We both had to hold back a snort. In that instant, the whole conversation had become a farce, and we were just puppets playing out the "man reports a crime" scenario, which went nowhere and meant nothing.

The alderman's office did the glad-handing thing, and was more polite than the desk sergeant at the precinct, but ultimately it was a whole lot of fancy words to cover up the line, "are you serious with this shit?"

Both the cops and the politicians were thinking the same thing: *There are real problems in this city, dude, and real criminals to catch, and you're trying to get us to provide resources to find out who's drawing dicks on your bathroom wall? Fuck you, buddy.* Hell, I am embarrassed to bring it up, but I don't know what else to do, here.

Sergeant Rodriguez tried to be helpful on a personal level, even if as a cop he was thinking that the sooner I leave, the sooner they could actually deal with crime. He suggested I buy a security system, maybe some cameras. I pointed out that the only thing I was worried about was happening inside the bathroom, and he pretty much told me that would be a sticky legal situation. There were really specific rules about where they could be placed, and ultimately, inside a stall was going to be a no-go for sure. Maybe a bathroom attendant, he said, someone to hand out condoms and breath-mints and keep an eye on things. That was the end of our conversation, I could tell. The period hung in the air like a fart.

After the cops, I headed toward the bar, like usual, but I tell you, this is really getting to me. I think I'm becoming paranoid. Do crazy people know they're crazy? You've got to wonder. These kids nod to me as I pass them on the street, just a couple of teenagers, whatever, but I imagine them staring at me as I pass them, so I stop and look back. Of course, the girl turns and looks over her shoulder and sees me standing there, jaw dropped, like some kind of pervert. She elbows her dude, and they walk a little faster, saying something shitty under their breath, speaking in whispers. I catch a glimpse of myself in a window nearby, and man, the dark circles under my eyes don't need high definition mirrors to shine back at me.

—DAY—
—LATER ON—

Someone carved, *For a bad time, call,* into the right side of
the stall partition. They didn't leave a number. They used a
knife. It's carved in, scraped the paint and the surface layer
of metal right off. It would be funny in any other circum-
stance, any other week.

— DAY 8 —

I had a dream last night.
I had a dream that scared the shit out of me.

I was in the bar, behind the counter, as usual, and there were a bunch of people inside, like we were having a party. There were elements of Mardi Gras all over the place. Eyeless, sparkling masks hung against the bar rail and beads were strewn everywhere, hanging off chairs and shelves. I looked down and saw that all across the bar, there were individual beads that had broken off a necklace. Purple, green, orange, all the colors, but one of the purple ones began to move on its own. It rolled down the counter, picking up speed. It was impossible to catch, like a fly, just ahead of where a hand would be to stop its momentum.

The bead skipped like a billiard ball and flipped onto the floor. I followed it across the boards, crouching down so as not to lose it. Slowly, it came to a halt in the middle of the floor, where I could finally grab it. It was cold, almost icy to the touch, like it had been inside the freezer. All around me were these dancers. I couldn't really see what they were wearing, even though I was looking right at them. It was like, everyone was made of a shadow, or like the illustrations on that old public access show Mystery or something. Silhouettes of top hats and fancy ball gowns from some other place and time, but almost cardboard cutouts instead of people. Each couple was locked in step together, circling and spiraling around me.

The bar was missing. Instinct told me I was still inside the bar, but there were no tables, no chairs, no jukebox or dart board or familiar counter. The room was empty, which at the same time made it full of all the potential of a space that hasn't congealed into anything just yet. If this wasn't my bar, it could have been any number of other things. I remembered a string of words that came out of my mouth, then: The space would yield to the dominant will exerted. The dancers, faceless shadows all turned inward, surrounding me, shifting in time with the music. I told them it was time to go home. "This is not your reality. You want the one next door." I yelled that, like a lunatic, and then everyone around me just faded out like old photographs. In my mind, I knew they left through the door, but where was the door?

It's odd, in dreams, how things can hold multiple different meanings all at once. A stranger can also be your boss and your grandma and your third-grade teacher and a snake, all at the same time, and every single self is valid and real in that dream logic kind of way.

The same confusion between my perception and the story I'd been somehow able to observe from outside myself happened again, then. I'd walked out the door, which had apparently been there the whole time, even though I just saw it now.

My key was soft, like it was a child's toy version of my front door key, and I was on the street outside my bar, but it was also some patch of woods, and I knew this somehow, even though I couldn't see the trees. I locked the door and then without even turning around, I was walking on a dark forest path.

I started running along the path, knowing I was moving toward home, but clouds were rolling through a deep purple sky much faster than they were supposed to go, and when I looked back down, the buildings were gone, and there was a stream in front of me. A few feet ahead of me, a little girl was skipping along. She remained the same distance away from me regardless of my speed, and no matter how she turned with the wax and wane of the stream's direction, her face was always turned away from me, and I felt this sense of fear and longing and emotions I don't know how to describe.

But I followed this little girl.

She asked me, "What's it like?"

My rational mind, whatever part of it was working, or maybe knew this was a dream, meant to ask, "What's what like?" but I heard different words come out of my mouth and they were: "It's not like anything you wrote. It's more sincere than that."

Now it was getting dark, and she was moving faster, getting a little further away from me.

I sped up. There was something in me that was screaming, "Don't let her leave you here alone. Don't ever be alone in the woods. Bad things happen when she leaves you alone."

So I tried to catch up, but in dreams sometimes your limbs won't cooperate with what you tell them to do. I felt all my muscles contract and tense as I pushed forward, trying to run, trying to close the distance gap between this girl and me, and now the clouds had become a freeway above us and the blue was a dull reddish purple, but she was still getting farther away.

It was like fighting through a cage filled with molasses. She stopped and looked out over the river. The other shore was missing its trees, and then the blank spaces were long wooden poles, like the handles of shovels. I knew they were grave stones. Then I was floating over myself, watching myself, in two places at once, and I was floating face down in the water. Somehow, I could see both the back of my body floating there like driftwood, and I also saw through my eyes to the bottom of the river.

There was a face staring up at me. It was the same little

girl, but I didn't know her. Her eyes were open and locked with mine, even though she was buried in the mud of the river bottom so that only her face was exposed. She looked calm, and just watched me. I knew that if I opened my mouth, I'd drown, but I couldn't lift my head, because it was suddenly very heavy. No part of me could be moved. I couldn't struggle. I couldn't right myself. And then, I saw one of her hands break the muddy surface, her fingers wriggling like worms and I knew what was about to happen. Her mouth suddenly opened up, and a rush of bubbles filled my view and I felt a grip on my wrist like an undertow.

The feeling of being grabbed wakes me up. I yelp like a wounded dog, startled at the sound of my own noise, but my arms, my legs, my torso, everything is paralyzed. I find myself staring into the darkness, trying to calm down, and in those first few moments, as I'm shaking off the effects of sleep, there's someone in the darkness of my bedroom with me. I can just see the silhouette of something even blacker than the blackness, like paint that doesn't quite match because it's one shade off the original. It's a man. It's a tall man. Someone is in my apartment, and I feel my heart scream with rapid fire machine gun beats. I roar so loud it shreds my throat, and I throw myself out of bed toward whoever it is, my limbs coming online all of a sudden, but no. No, there's nothing. The shape breaks in two, a top and a bottom, sheared away from each other, and for a moment, there are two shorter figures, and then those shapes break up into smaller and smaller pieces and fade as I shake off the dream and realize that I really am awake.

I've never had a heart attack, but I am sure I am having one now. I lay there against my bed frame feeling my heart pound. I can feel it in my skull, like someone is drumming on my temples. I feel it in my stomach. My heart has never worked this hard. I am shaking, and I just sit, trembling on the floor, trying to figure out what has just happened.

I read this article that says talking about your dreams is kind of like an exorcism for your subconscious mind. The very act of writing it down, or talking about it, robs a dream of its power. Normally, I can't remember dreams, not like I could when I was a kid, but then I guess a lot of things change over time. This one, I can't seem to forget.

In that same article about dreams, they'd written about sleep paralysis, where you wake up in the middle of the night and can't move. Some people actually feel like they're falling backward into their own body as they wake up, which a lot of people think is where astral projection stories come from. There's this feeling of being outside yourself, and not able to control anything, and being robbed of that agency in your own body is the worst horror your unconscious mind can possibly throw at you.

So I write it all down. I didn't sleep after that. I couldn't. I turn on the lights and watch some movies for a while. But now, even after putting it all down on paper, the images are just burned into my retinas. I can't stop seeing that little girl's face. What's worse is, as I'm writing this, something I've been trying not to dwell on, but it's true, so I guess I have to think about. You know how I'd said before that sometimes you know things mean more than one thing in a dream? That strange little girl didn't look like anyone I knew, and there had been nothing recognizable about her at all. Not even a little bit. But somehow, I'd known, in my heart of hearts, I known that it was my sister Donnie.

Shit. I have to call her.

— DAY 9 —

BLAM. Like a rifle shot.

3:48 AM.

I remember the time. I guess because it's the only thing I could see in the dark. Those glowing numbers, and me wondering why I was awake hours before I needed to be.

Weird thing is, I can sleep through just about anything if it's big enough. Thunder, tornadoes with their air raid sirens, barking dogs, heavy bass in a car driving by my windows at night, nothing wakes me up. Somehow, my sleeping brain knows those things are outside, and I'm safe in my space. But, if something small happens inside my space, it triggers a fight or flight response and my eyes snap open. It can be as small as my mom closing my door in the morning when I was a kid, and still sleeping on a Saturday morning. Just that delicate hiss of the door bottom brushing against the carpet would wake me. When I've had pets, same deal. The cat pads across the floor and I feel the switch flip and I'm up, totally aware of the world around me.

The crash that woke me up combines a massive noise with the close proximity of my space being invaded and I bolt up. This is the second night in a row I've woken up with my heart beating so fast it's about to explode. I nearly hyperventilated, but I start doing my square breathing again, to slow down my heart rate and catch my breath.

My mind spins around and around, trying to discern what could have made a noise like that. There isn't much heavy in my place that could have fallen, and it doesn't sound like a tree or anything from the outside. But then, as I slowly inhaled and exhaled, it triggers the memory from the other day. The last time I was doing this. I'd been dreaming.

I had been under the bedroom, inside the crawlspace.

My nerves shatter and I instinctively clutch at the covers and tear the sheets untucked until they are swaddling my shoulders. I look down, like I can somehow stare through the mattress and into the hollow space beneath the floorboards. The sound that woke me. It sounded exactly like a wooden trapdoor falling shut.

I hadn't been inside the crawlspace in a really long time. Years, maybe. There was nothing down there but pipes and electrics these days. When I'd first moved in, I kept camping equipment and outdoor stuff down there. There was a plumbing problem, some kind of leak or break in the pipes, and everything down there got soaked. Once the plumber had fixed everything, I emptied it out, inserted some three-inch screws to keep it secure, and now I didn't really think about it.

There is nothing else that could have made that sound. It takes every bit of life left in me to check. I know I would never sleep again until I see for myself that everything in the house is exactly as I'd left it before I fell asleep. The blaze of my mag-light fills the room like a white star, when I bring it out from under my bed and arm myself with its reassuring heft. It's a big old 300 lumen LED monster with a sturdy metal handle and textured grip. A club with blinding light shooting out one end. Like a throwback to primitive man, where the end of the club was lit up to ward off predators.

Every single light in the house comes on as I walked through, my hands fumbling blindly in the dark for anything that might serve as a safety net to set my jangled nerves to rest. As I creep down the hall and peer around the corner, I don't know what I expect to see, but in that moment, in that state, it really could have been anything.

A burglar, a neighbor, a long dead relative, a nightmare monster here to kill me and devour me. All things seem possible and just as likely as anything else.

Instead, what I see is the room that serves as my cleaning closet and pantry, undisturbed. I have to move some cardboard boxes filled with old clothes and blankets and pull up the rug to see it, but the door is there just like usual. The screws are still tight, nearly flush against the wood despite the fact that I'd had to tow-nail them in at an angle. I pull at the door, and it doesn't even rattle.

It's funny. I laugh at myself. I haven't let bad dreams upset me like this since I was a little kid. As I am putting the rug back, it occurs to me that there are two lines in the dust on the edge where the rug lives. It takes me a minute to talk myself out of my growing paranoia. I had to have made another line when I moved the rug as I checked on the door. There's just no other explanation for it, since this thing hasn't been moved in months, maybe over a year.

It is 4:20 AM by the time I crawl back into bed.

I see it turn 4:30. Then 5:00, 6:00 and then at 6:30, with the first rays of light breaking through my blinds, I say, fuck it. and make myself a cup of coffee. As I wait for it to brew, I stand in the doorway of the pantry and stare at that spot. I can't remember whether or not I'd put the boxes back, but it appears that I haven't, as they are scattered all over the place. The rug is right where I had left it, but now it is impossible to tell where it had been even as recently as yesterday. It's impossible to keep track, anymore.

I read this story about a Japanese woman in the news, who lived for months and months where she would find little things around her home had been moved or gone missing. Rice would disappear, or some personal item would be on the left side of her dresser when she was sure she'd left it on the right side. At first, she thought maybe she had mice or something, but there was no evidence, no scat, nothing except these weird little peculiarities.

She would get the feeling sometimes, when she was

home alone, that she was being watched, or that some presence was near. This woman didn't believe in hauntings or ghosts, but she was running out of rational explanations.

Turns out, totally unknown to her, there had been a man living inside one of her cabinets for a year. He'd sneak out at night, or while the woman was at work, otherwise he'd hide there, a secret and silent partner participating in her every waking moment. Can you imagine all the things this stranger saw and heard? Can you imagine what an intrusion that would be? How psychically violated she felt when she discovered that this man had been intensely close to her for that long, and how many times she probably walked right by him, only an inch or two of solid matter between them and an accidental cough away from a confrontation or a heart attack?

Telltale heart. Beating under the floorboards. If someone is living under my place, they're stuck there. Those screws aren't moving. I can't keep track of my ghosts. Maybe I'm the one doing the haunting.

— DAY 10 —

I left it alone last night. I know I did. After I spoke with the cops and everything, I decided I'd just leave it. I'm tired of cleaning up someone else's mess anyway. Until we get to the bottom of this, it can just sit there.

It changed.

How the hell is this happening? It was brand new words today, not the same as when I left them there. How?

IT WAS ONLY THE SUMMER BEFORE. WHAT A DIFFERENCE ONE YEAR CAN MAKE. AN ETERNITY.

DONNIE HAD BROUGHT ONE OF MOM'S KITCHEN KNIVES, A SMALL PARING KNIFE, USED FOR CUTTING TOMATOES, NOW CONJURING A DIFFERENT

SHADE OF RED. I CAREFULLY CARVED A SCARLET HALF-MOON IN THE CENTER OF MY PALM, FEELING THE FLAP OF SKIN COME AWAY WITH A HINT OF RELUCTANCE. A DARK DROP BUBBLED UP, THE SURFACE TENSION HOLDING IT TOGETHER. SHE LOOKED AT THE GLOBE IN THE MIDDLE OF MY PALM.

"IT LOOKS LIKE A RUBY."

"COME ON, IT'S YOUR TURN."

I HANDED HER THE KNIFE, HANDLE FIRST. HER SMALL HAND SWALLOWED IT, THE

BLADE JUTTING OUT, ASKEW, THE TINIEST STAIN SHINING ON THE POINT. SHE HESITATED, TURNING THE BLADE IN THE MORNING SUN. A FLASH OF THE BLADE BLINDED ME MOMENTARILY AND LEFT A BLUE SHADOW IMPRESSION WHEN I BLINKED.

"I ALREADY PROMISED. I DON'T WANT TO DO THIS."

"A PROMISE DOESN'T MEAN ANYTHING. IT'S JUST WORDS. THIS IS DIFFERENT. THIS IS BLOOD. THIS MEANS SOMETHING."

DONNIE PRESSED THE FLAT EDGE OF THE KNIFE AGAINST HER PALM AND SQUINTED. HER PAIN RESPONSE WAS PREMATURE, THE FEAR IN HER EYES FLASHING BEFORE THE NERVES TRIGGERED. WE LOCKED EYES FOR A MOMENT, AND I NODDED TO HER THROUGH THE ELECTRIC BLUE HAZE OF SPOTS CRAWLING ACROSS HER T-ZONE.

WE SPOKE THE WORDS WE HAD DECIDED UPON TOGETHER. "WE WILL HAVE NO FEAR. WE WILL PROTECT EACH OTHER. IT IS US AGAINST THE WORLD, AND WE ARE IN IT TOGETHER NO MATTER WHAT."

A SQUEAK. SHE SHUT HER EYES FOR JUST A MOMENT AS THE BLADE BIT, A TINY RED WEAL APPEARING LIKE A CRACK IN THE EARTH. WE PRESSED BLOOD TO MAGMA, FEELING THE TICKLE OF OPEN WOUNDS DANCING. BLOOD THAT SHARED A GENETIC MEMORY, BINDING TOGETHER AND UNDERSTANDING THAT IT HAD FOUND A LOST PART OF ITSELF. I GRABBED HER HAND WITH MY OWN AND SHOOK IT LIKE I'D SEEN MY FATHER DO. A FIRM SHAKE, ONLY TWO PUMPS, TENDONS SHIMMYING IN MY FOREARM AS I PRESSED HARDER.

"NOW, YOU CAN'T CHANGE

YOUR MIND. WE'RE BOUND.
THIS IS FOREVER. NO JOKE."

A BRAVE AND PROUD MASK
FELL OVER HER FACE AND
SHE HISSED. "MMM HMM. LET
GO, NOW."

PERHAPS IF I'D BEEN ABLE
TO SEE PAST THE GLINTING
AFTER IMAGES BURNED INTO
MY CORNEAS, I WOULD HAVE
READ A DIFFERENT TALE,
BUT FOR NOW THIS WOULD
DO.

I WAS FAR TOO NAIVE FOR
THE IDEA OF THIS BEING A
GAME TO EVEN ENTER MY

MIND. THIS WAS BLOOD MAGIC, THE CHAOS OF A UNIVERSE I DID NOT UNDERSTAND HOW TO FIT INTO BALLED UP, CRUSHED, AND SQUEEZED INTO THE PALM OF MY HAND BY THE PERSON I TRUSTED MOST IN THE WORLD. THE AFTERMATH TOOK THIS RITUAL AND TWISTED IT INTO SOMETHING BROKEN. THERE WAS NO FOREVER LEFT. ONLY THE MEMORY OF SOMETHING HAVING BEEN IMPORTANT AND ITS FAILURE TO BIND. A PROTON AND A NEUTRON LOSING THEIR GRIP AND ALLOWING THE ELECTRON THEY HAD IN COMMON TO TRANSCEND THE BOUNDARY OF THEIR LOVE AND SEPARATE THEM.

I HAD NO WAY OF KNOWING
THIS.

YOU'D CALL ME SELFISH
FOR THINKING THAT THERE
ARE SORTS OF BINDINGS
IMPOSSIBLE TO SEVER.
FAMILIAL BONDS ARE ONE
SUCH TYPE, AS ARE OATHS
SWORN IN SERVICE AND LOVE.
HOW COULD I KNOW, IN MY
YOUTH AND INEXPERIENCE,
THAT WE WERE ADRIFT,
DESTINED TO FLOAT OUR
HANDS OUT OF THE RANGE TO
INTERLOCK FINGERS SIMPLY
BY VIRTUE OF GROWING
UP? IT WAS IMPOSSIBLE
FOR ME TO CONCEIVE OF A
WORLD WHERE WE WEREN'T
THIS CLOSE FOREVER AND

ALWAYS. IN ALL THE INFINITE POSSIBILITIES OF LIFE, THIS HAD TO BE A CERTAINTY. DONNIE WAS MY SISTER, BUT SHE WAS MY IDOL, MY ROCK, MY COUNSELOR AND MY SAGE. I HAD NOBODY ELSE TO TAKE HER PLACE AS SHE FOUND NEW PASTURES TO ROAM AND AGED INTO WOMANHOOD. TO HER, I WAS CERTAIN IT FELT NATURAL, AN EVOLUTION OF THE SELF NO DIFFERENT THAN ANY OTHER BURGEONING ADOLESCENCE. TO ME, ON THE OTHER HAND, THE LARGEST ARTERY PUMPING BLOOD INTO MY HEART HAD BECOME THIN, BLOCKED, ATROPHIED, AND I COULD NO LONGER HEAR A BEAT, BUT

ONLY THE ANGRY BUZZING OF
MY OWN UNCONTROLLABLE
THOUGHTS.

— DAY 11 —

I called Donnie this morning, just to catch up. She sounded surprised to hear from me. I guess it has been a while. I don't like talking on the phone very often. I get plenty of talking done at the bar, and I don't really like the impersonal touch of talking to some disembodied voice on a chirping brick. It makes my ear hot. But, it was nice to hear her voice, especially with everything that's been happening lately. Sometimes, you have to turn to family. Blood.

There'd been some part of me, despite knowing better, that expected her to not answer the phone. Or worse, I would hear the phone pick up, and there'd be just this breathing, wheezing, gasping, choking sound. When words come, they would come slow and painful, wrung out through lips ragged and chapped with stress. "Someone is in the house," she'd say, or "I'm trapped, you have to call the police," or maybe even just a death rattle. Or the sound of someone struggling to breathe. I think that's what I'm really afraid of. The wrong kind of answer. One that tears me apart, like my nightmares.

What the hell am I afraid of, exactly?

To my relief, it had started like any other conversation.

I asked how she was doing, and she told me she was good.

"How's your husband? Kids?"

"They're great. Ellen is doing dance classes now, so that's new. She keeps us busy running her around. Danny is really getting into building stuff now, Lego and that kind of stuff. He built some Star Wars ships the other day that looked like they might actually fly. I warned him not to take them up on the roof to try them out. You never know with that kid. How are you? How's life treating you?"

How life's been treating me? I'm not sure.

"I'm fine. Good. Business as usual around here."

"That's good."

"Yeah, still fighting the good fight."

"You need new curtains in that bar. Something to make it look more homey."

"Maybe so."

There's a silence then, for a second. This one second, my internal sense of time stretches and deforms. It lasts for what feels like minutes. It's stage time, compressed beyond recognition and then blown out so far it no longer feels like time, but unrecognizable fragments of some mystery the brain can't fathom.

She breaks it, like a cold splash of water in the face.

"You sound like you haven't been sleeping well."

There's no answer for that. Nothing comes to mind. No words on the tip of my tongue. I just breathe into the phone, listening to the echo of my own exhale.

"You still there?' she asks me.

"Yeah, sorry."

She can tell something's wrong, but she can't tell what it is. Neither can I.

"The kids are getting bigger. You really ought to come see them."

I promise that I should, not that I will, and neither of us mention the difference. She goes back to a comfortable place, her family. Danny's in third grade now and playing team sports in addition to his building interests. Ellen is taking dance classes and she's just about to enter some kind of academy for high school kids who have an interest in the arts. I don't bother to mention that she's already updated me on the dancing. It's treading over familiar ground because all of a sudden there's an awkward chasm that's opened up in the ground between us, and neither of us can see the bottom of it or quite know why it's there.

"Walt is still working for the construction company, but I guess he got a promotion a few months back, so now he's mostly behind a desk in an office instead of down at the sites he oversees."

"Good for him."

"You sound so tired. Or, sick, maybe? Is something the matter?"

For some reason, I'm finding this whole situation ridiculous now. I start thinking about the story and the dreams and all this hoodoo shit that's been weirding me out, and I just start laughing.

"What's funny?" she asks me.

I'll find a way to confess. I never could keep much from my sister, to my recollection. She has a way of pushing needles under my skin until I tell told her what I'm not telling her. So, I tell her:

"I don't know, there's this story that some idiot is writing in my bathroom stalls, and it had me a little freaked out."

She laughs. Of course she laughs. It's so dumb.

"Is it dirty?" she asks me.

"No, it's not dirty. What kind of place do you think I run?"

She laughs, and in a mean voice, the kind only a little sister can wield like a battle ax, she says "I don't know, I think last time you showed me that place I saw a glory hole."

"Butt face." Suddenly, I feel like we're kids again, only talking through this god damned electric brick instead of face to butt face.

"It's just weird is all, it sounds like a crime story or something. Some guy walking behind a girl, and there's a murder, and it was your name they used, Donnie, so I guess that freaked me out a little."

She sighs into the phone. "It's not that rare a name."

I sputter, trying to keep talking. My mouth is dry. "This

guy and this girl are walking by the crick, and they're skipping stones, and then he ends up jumping on top of her and trying to drown her in the water, and he holds her underwater until she stops breathing. Really brutal stuff. Then there's this stuff about him running through the woods after that, but man, it was just... the way it was written. Really unsettling. At first, I was thinking someone was confessing to a murder in my restroom. Crazy, huh?"

There's total silence at the other end of the line. You can hear a pin drop. Then, I hear her exhale. She must have been holding her breath.

"Do you want to hear the rest? Are you there?" I ask, just to make sure she's still into the story and I'm not boring her, but she just makes this choking sound. I flash back to the paranoid delusions I was feeling when I was listening to the ring. The catch in her throat was alien and unwelcome.

"What? Why would you—?" she asks me. She didn't finish it.

"Why would I what?" I ask. The feeling in my gut tells me I did something wrong, that I crossed some invisible line into territory I'm not supposed to visit. I can feel my eyebrows knitting together, as I am perplexed, confused, anxious. What just happened?

"I have to go," she mumbles.

"Already?"

"Leave it behind."

That's it. The call was cut off. I'm pretty sure that's what she said, but I didn't get a chance to ask her to repeat it. The next thing I know, I hear the phone click off, and there's nothing. The electric hiss of connection disappears. Okay, I'm thinking, weird, but maybe we just got cut off or something happened, so I call her back, but she doesn't answer. It just goes straight to her voice mail.

"Hey, Donnie... we must have gotten disconnected somehow. It was really nice talking to you. Call me back some time, or when you get this, or whenever. Give my love to Walt and the kids, and don't be a stranger. We really should talk more often." I pause there, not sure what else to say. I hate messages. They always ramble on way too long and have so little substance you might have been better off not saying anything at all. I feel like I need to speak some magic word though, some hidden phrase that will unlock the secrets of the awkwardness I had just experienced. I finally figure it out, something to stab with, and I'm just about to say, "Sorry if I freaked you out, I didn't mean to," and then maybe continue on from there, but the thing beeps and my attempt at communication is over.

I don't call back a third time. I just sit there, cold, thinking about what just happened and what it meant, and wonder if anything means anything, in the end.

— DAY 12 —

The bar is closed. I'm not opening today. I call Cher and
tell her not to worry about coming in. Tell her I'll pay her
half a day just to stay home. I'd come in today because I
don't have anywhere else that feels like home, not even my
actual home. But I get in here this morning, and I catch a
glimpse of myself in the bar mirror, and christ, I don't look
good. Stubble sticking out of my face at odd angles like the
legs of insects.

    I'd left it in place last night. I didn't wash it off.
    It's changed.
    Like it has always been this way.
    Like I never did anything at all.

THE LOCUST CEASELESSLY
BUZZES ON, DEVOURING FROM
WITHIN. THEY'VE TRIED TO
EXTERMINATE IT, BRINGING
POISONOUS WORDS TO BEAR,
SMOKING THE HIVE OUT WITH
CHOKING, PROBING CONFUSION,
APPLYING MIND GAMES LIKE WAR
PAINT, AND YET IT LIVES ON.

WE PLAY DRESS-UP TOGETHER, STANDING LIKE GODS UNDERNEATH CRIMSON SKIES THAT DRIP WITH THE ODOR OF SACRED HERBS. THEY DO NOT SEE US. NOBODY SEES US, ALMOST, BUT THEN, A BEACON. ONE SEEING THROUGH THE VEIL, INTO WHAT COULD HAVE BEEN, AND WHAT NEVER WAS, AND SUDDENLY THERE WAS SILENCE AND DOUBT.

TAKE OFF YOUR MANTLE PIECE. LET THE EARTH CRUMBLE. YOUR BOOTS ARE MUDDY, GASHED ACROSS YOUR ACHILLES TENDONS WITH A MACHETE. A FLESH TOWER LEFT WITHOUT A

MIND TO CONTROL VARIABLES,
REACTING WITH ANIMAL
INSTINCT IN THE MARSHES OF
TIME.

THEYWATCHEVENNOW. THEY
PEEK OUT FROM BETWEEN
COAT BUTTONS, LAPPING UP
MOLTEN GOLD THAT DRIPS
FROM BENEATH THE SPINE
OF HEAVEN. THEY SELL YOU
INTO SLAVERY IN YOUR OWN
HOUSE. THEY OPEN UP LIKE
DOORS. THEY LAY IN WAIT
BENEATH, BREATHING IN
THE FIBERGLASS PARTICLES
AND LUXURIATING IN THE
COUGHING EMBRACE OF
ABSCESSED LUNGS.

EVEN THE WAY HOME CAN NO LONGER BE WITNESSED. THE LABYRINTH WITH ENDLESS SOLUTIONS ENCASES US IN AN AMBER OF OPTION PARALYSIS. OUR WINGS SHIVER, TWITCH, LAST VESTIGES OF OBEDIENCE TO THE SELF BOWING BEFORE THE INEVITABLE MARCH OF ENTROPY.

I COUNT MY LEGS. THERE ARE SIX. THEN FOUR. THEN TWO. FIRST, I SEE THE INSECT, THE BRITTLE, SHARP BLADED KNEES IN EACH SPINDLY APPENDAGE. THEN, I SEE SHE AND I, HUDDLED TOGETHER, PLAYING, COSTUMED, EACH USING WHAT WE HAVE TO INHABIT HALF OF THE WHOLE.

NEXT, I SEE MYSELF, ALONE, WALKING, GRACELESS, DRIPPING WET WITH RIVER WATER, UNABLE TO FIND MY HOME. LAST, I SEE NO LEGS AT ALL, A SERPENT'S SLITHERING PATH THROUGH THE GARDEN, A FALL FROM GRACE, A LOSS OF INNOCENCE, SILKY SMOOTH DEBASEMENT AND IT TASTES LIKE LIQUID CANDY AS I LOSE MYSELF IN A SPIRAL OF ENVY AND GUILT.

THERE'SNOTHINGLEFTHERE. WE WILL MOVE AWAY. WE WILL FORGET OUR PAST. WE WILL WEAVE A NEW FUTURE, SNIPPING THE ROOTS THAT CLING TO OUR ANKLES AND

DRAG US BACK THROUGH MEMORY, TRYING TO DROWN US IN THE SOIL. THERE IS NO SWIMMING AGAINST THE CURRENT. THERE IS NO FORGIVENESS. THERE IS NO SALVATION HERE. MAYBE SOMEWHERE ELSE, THERE IS SOMETHING THAT COULD RESEMBLE IT, IN THE RIGHT LIGHT, IF WE SQUINT JUST HARD ENOUGH TO MAKE OUR EYEBALLS BURST.

I'm scared. I don't know what's happening anymore, and I'm fucking terrified.

Someone stopped by earlier, maybe an hour ago. It might have been Mookie and the fellas, but I don't know. I didn't look. I sat here behind the counter, watching the shadows wander around outside the two little windows in the front by the door. They're colored in, like stained glass, so it's difficult to see anything detailed through them. Someone presses their face up against one of the windows, trying to see in. A shadowy finger taps on the glass. I just sit there, staring at my reflection, now all warped and twisted in the side of a cocktail shaker.

After what seems like forever, the shadows back away,

becoming formless. It's not like me to close without at least putting a sign on the door. It's not like me to get paranoid and start muttering under my breath and see things that aren't there out of the corner of my eye. I can't believe I'm this paranoid. It's stupid. The guilt about feeling so ridiculous just perpetuates the cycle. I'm feeling low and homicidal and raw. I must smell like garbage. I know I look like it. I stand up and throw the rag down. My eyes are itchy. They want to cry, and I don't understand why.

I'm standing there, thinking these disgusting thoughts about myself, when I hear a buzzing sound. A low hum, like someone is shaking a can of peas very gently or maybe the clearing of a bird's throat, just this weird thrumming sound. I admit it, I know I've been going a little off the rails, but I can't help it. Writing it down had been helping, but now I feel like maybe it's feeding this disease or whatever is happening here. But this humming is constant, and as I listen, my ears finally track it and focus in, and I know deep in my heart of hearts that this sound is coming from the bathroom.

My nine-millimeter Beretta is in a lockbox hidden underneath the front bar. I fall on my ass trying to stay quiet— stupid—and I crawl underneath the bar. It's all instinct. I've put so much time and life into this place, it feels like an extension of me, so it takes me no time to slip the key out of my pocket and into the box. Before I turn it though, as I lie here behind the bar, I feel my eyes begin to close. I'm fighting sleep. I haven't been sleeping well, and although my senses are heightened and on fire with the idea of danger, some part of me says "forget it, just go to sleep." I feel like I haven't had a decent night for a week or more. Maybe I haven't. Drifting in and out of consciousness, watching the digital clock change from one hazy, foreign symbol to the next, the sounds of my own body switching positions in the dark until I'm halfway off the bed, limbs dangling— these are the only things that night has been providing me.

No, this is crazy, I think to myself, I'm in danger. My

life is in danger. Something or someone is here, and sleep is death. But reality has been so hard to pin down recently, and as I'm thinking about the danger and the terror, I realize I'm laying my head down on the filthy but soft rubber mat and it feels so perfect. The sound is white noise, blocking thoughts and seducing me into closing my eyes and just letting the vibration fill up the space between my ears.

It's warm, and the wooden floor under the mat provides a cradle and I find myself thinking "so what if I did just go to sleep?" I wonder if I would ever wake up? Maybe something would happen. Maybe not. Maybe I'd wake up and find out I'd been asleep for all of this, this whole diary, this is all just dream logic, and when I wake up, there's no book at all and everything makes perfect sense. Or maybe the person or thing that has been carving stories into my space will murder me while I sleep and I'll just slip away.

I DREAMED OF DROWNING.

I WAS PLAYING IN THE TREES, SNAPPING OFF BRANCHES AND WHIPPING THEM THROUGH THE AIR LIKE SWITCHES AGAINST THE TRUNKS. MY BARE FEET GRIPPED THICK BRANCHES, A THROWBACK TO SOME ANCIENT ANCESTOR BEFORE

WE CAME DOWN FROM THE FOLIAGE.

WHEN I HESITATED FOR JUST A MOMENT, I BECAME AWARE THAT I WAS FALLING. MY INNER EAR BUZZED, MY STOMACH SEIZED, AND MY GAZE PULLED BACK LIKE A CAMERA AS I WATCHED THE BRANCHES ABOVE ME DISAPPEAR. THEN, BLUE, EVERYWHERE, AND A CRACKING SENSATION AS I HIT THE SURFACE OF THE WATER. THE WATER RUSHED OVER ME, PULLING MY BODY DEEPER, UNAFFECTED BY MY HORRIFIED ATTEMPTS TO RIGHT MYSELF.

THE RIVER BED WAS NO LONGER BELOW ME. AN ABYSS YAWNED BELOW LIKE AN OCEANIC TRENCH. KICKING FRANTICALLY SERVED ONLY TO SPIN ME AROUND IN A CIRCLE, AND SOMEHOW, I ENDED UP FACING DOWN ONCE MORE. THE LIGHT WAS FADING, BUT THERE WAS SOME KIND OF UNNATURAL LIGHT DOWN HERE. IT SEEMED THAT MY BODY WAS GLOWING WITH SOME FAINT LIGHT THAT ALLOWED ME TO SEE A FEW FEET IN EVERY DIRECTION, BUT BEYOND MY LITTLE GLOBE, A DARK VOID SURROUNDED EVERYTHING.

MY LUNGS ACHED. I KEPT BREATHING, EVEN UNDERWATER, BY SOME METHOD UNKNOWN TO ME, BUT IT WAS STRAINED, PAINFUL AND AWKWARD. IT WAS DIFFICULT TO EXPLAIN, BUT IT REMINDED ME OF BREATHING THROUGH A HEAVY BLANKET, OR MAYBE WHEN A BIG DOG SITS ON YOUR CHEST WHILE YOU TRY TO GULP AIR.

IN THE INKY BLACK AROUND MY CIRCLE, I KEPT GLIMPSING BURSTS OF MOTION, SOME SHADOW DIVING DOWN BELOW OR FLOATING JUST OUTSIDE OF VISIBILITY. SOMETHING BRUSHED AGAINST THE HAIR

ON THE BACK OF MY NECK,
BUT WHEN I WHIPPED AROUND
IN A PANIC, THERE WAS
NOTHING THERE. JUST THE
SAME FADED BLUISH GLOW
OBFUSCATING ANY DETAILS
THAT WEREN'T DIRECTLY A
PART OF ME.

THE SURFACE OF THE RIVER
WAS LONG GONE. IT HAD
BECOME AN OCEAN. THERE
WAS NO BANK, OR BOTTOM,
JUST THIS ENDLESS, SLOW
DESCENT.

I KNOW DREAMS TAKE ONLY
MOMENTS TO PASS, BUT THEY
FEEL LIKE FOREVER, AND
THIS FELT LIKE FOREVER

INDEFINITELY. MY BREATHING HAD SLOWED, BUT EVERY INHALATION STILL FELT LIKE A STRUGGLE TO LIVE. THE WATER WAS GETTING COLDER. I HAD NO IDEA HOW FAR DOWN I'D GOTTEN.

THAT'S WHEN I HEARD SOMEONE CALL MY NAME.

RIGHT NEXT TO MY EAR.

MY STOMACH NEARLY RUPTURED AND I TRIED TO SCREAM, BUT NOTHING CAME OUT. I TURNED MY HEAD AS FAST AS I COULD. IT FELT LIKE PUSHING A BOULDER

UP A HILL. THEN I HEARD IT AGAIN, FROM FURTHER AWAY, ON THE OTHER SIDE OF MY HEAD. IT WAS MY NAME. IT WAS A SMALL VOICE. AN ECHO. A BREEZE. AND IT MADE ME SO TERRIFIED I WANTED TO DIE.

MY EYES WOULDN'T SHUT. DREAM LOGIC. MY REAL EYES, MIGHT BE CLOSED, MIGHT NOT, IN MY BED, BUT HERE, I JUST HAD TO STARE INTO THE NOTHING. I THOUGHT ABOUT ALL THE WAYS I MIGHT BE ABLE TO WAKE MYSELF, PINCHING, OR TRYING TO FALL OR HIT MYSELF IN THE HEAD, BUT THERE WAS NOTHING. I DIDN'T

HAVE CONTROL ANYMORE.
MY HANDS WERE STIFF, AND
I SAW SCARS ALL OVER THEM.
A NICE BIG ONE RIGHT IN THE
MIDDLE OF EACH PALM MADE
ME BREATHE FASTER. MY
LUNGS WERE ON FIRE.

I SUDDENLY LANDED ON
A VAST, WHITE SURFACE.
THE GROUND WAS SANDY,
LIKE SOME KIND OF HUGE
UNDERWATER SHOAL. AS
MY FEET DUG IN, I FELT
SOMETHING SOFT AND COLD
UNDERNEATH THE SAND.
SOMETHING SOLID.

THEN ALL OF A SUDDEN,
I'M OUTSIDE MYSELF, THE

CAMERA IS PULLING BACK, AND I SEE MYSELF STANDING THERE, GETTING SMALLER AND AS MY VIEW PANS OUT, I FEEL MYSELF TRY TO SCREAM AGAIN, AND BUBBLES FLOAT IN FRONT OF ME, EVEN THOUGH MY BODY IS STANDING DOWN THERE ON THIS... THING.

IT GOES ON AND ON, THE BIGGEST MASS OF FLESH I'VE EVER SEEN, GRAVESTONE WHITE IN THIS ENDLESS BLACKNESS. FAR BENEATH WHERE I'M STANDING—NOW STARTING TO SINK—THE WHITENESS MOVES AROUND LIKE LIQUID THROUGH VEINS, A PULPY MASS SHIFTING

AROUND UNCERTAINLY, IN
INTESTINAL KNOTS.

"GEORGIE."

"WHAT?"

"GEORGIE."

"WHAT IS IT?"

"I'M RIGHT HERE."

"WHERE?"

"DOWN HERE."

"HERE?"

"WHERE YOU LEFT ME."

I wake up to the sizzling frequency buzz whine of one of the bar lights. Only one is on. One ivory white bar of electric lightning flickering above me, from just on the other side of the counter. It vibrates on and off. It sounds like the chainsaw buzz of an insect. I scratch and claw for memories, trying to shake off a groggy post-nap confusion. What time is it? I have no idea. I can't reach my phone, and I can't see the bar clock. Wrong angle. Too dark.

The corner where my lips meet is moist and encrusted with dried saliva. I wonder how long I'd been out. This isn't the first time I've slept at the bar, but usually that involves setting up the futon in the back office and planning ahead.

I sniffle. There's a tiny pain in my nose, and moisture on my upper lip. I poke at my nostril with my index finger and it stings a little. There's blood on the tip, partly dried and crusty brown. I reach around for the switch I know is under the bar and flick it on.

A thin neon blue casts weird shadows, a forest of bottles cascading over my arms. Still, it's more constant than the faded flicker of the emergency lights. The shiny steel martini shaker reveals that my nose had been bleeding. I can still taste copper in the back of my throat. I leave a dirty rust-colored stain on a clean bar rag and sit up. My vision clears even as I fight off the groggy wobbling feeling above my shoulders. Naps usually don't do me much good, especially if they're fitful and unintended.

A sudden realization hits me that there is a weight in my hand. The lockbox has been opened. I am holding the gun, somehow retrieved while I'd been dreaming. I notice the safety is off, and my gut sinks into the floor. I am too groggy now to be dealing with firearms, and yet I do not put the gun away, because with sudden clarity, my ears focus like radar on the source of the hum. It isn't the lights above me, not entirely. That vibrating lullaby of sound waves that seems to almost hypnotize me is still creeping out from the bathroom, but now it sounds more frantic. The voltage got cranked up. I wonder if something had gone wrong with the fuses, but that's unlikely. Nothing is likely. That's why I carry the gun in front of me like a totem, to ward off any errant, wandering demons, as I crawl across the grime encrusted floor and press myself up against the wooden door to the men's room.

I open the bathroom door, just a crack, and the sound immediately increases in volume, like someone just cranked up a stereo. It's white noise, the kind that fancy people have those little bedside generators for. It's relaxing in other contexts, but here, it's threatening and weird and I have to remember to breathe. I stop breathing for what must have been a full minute. Is that even possible? I don't even know. If I could, I would call and ask a nurse to check on this.

There are no shoes showing underneath the stalls, as far as I can tell in the dim light shifting through the crack in the doorway. I figure if the criminal is in here, with this ray of light I'd just dropped into the space, they sure know I'm here now, so I reach up and slap at the light switch. The fluorescents take a second to kick on and then everything is illuminated. I'm low enough to the ground where I can see all the way to the wall. Nothing looks out of the ordinary. But, some part of me already knows. I know that sound, whatever it is, has to be coming from the stall with the story.

I decide to get it over with.

I stand up, and I scream like a wild man, letting out this fucking war whoop like an animal, and I charge the door. I barely get my fingers around the edge before I'm whipping the door open, and I'm already bringing the pistol up to bear on whoever is sitting there.

I don't give a shit if it's a man or a woman or a kid or a god damned ghost, I'm about to shoot it.

But, there ain't a thing there. Nothing. Except that buzz, which I now realize is coming from the stool. I'm looking into the water, and it's got a ripple to it, kind of like if a regular chain toilet is running with a broken chain, the water ripples slightly all the time. These are regular public fixtures though, just pipes and a pot, no tank to speak of. If these things break, they run like a firehose. So now I'm peering down into the hole, and I see something black edge out of the hole at the bottom.

I squint, and I look a little harder, and I freak the fuck out. I swear something just looked up at me, and I don't usually get the shakes from some nasty animal getting into human space. I mean, I've cleaned snakes out of gutters, and taken plenty of spiders out of bathroom showers in my day, but this is just so unexpected. This thing, it wriggles out, half drowned, and it looks like a grasshopper but black as night. Maybe some kind of oversized cricket.

Just when I'm thinking there's no way this thing could make that kind of noise unless it somehow chewed through a pipe, I see something wiggle its way forward right behind, and sure enough, it's another one. As I take a step back, already thinking about which exterminator to call, the buzzing amps up like I just shot a bee hive and these things start pushing their way out of the pipes, dozens of them. They're crawling up the inside of the toilet bowl, drowning each other to get out, legs pounding down heads, thorax stepladders.

Now there's an infestation, and I'm gagging and backing up as fast as I can. I hit the wall with my head. Chimes go ringing through my skull and my vision swims. It looks like there are a hundred of these things as I see the toilet vomit them up onto the tile with a series of chunky splashes.

I scramble backward out of the bathroom as fast as I can, screaming, falling all over myself, and when I get out to the bar, I break down crying. I'm watching the door, shaking like a leaf, ready to start firing my pistol at whatever crawls out of there, even though there is a part of me that knows this will be insane, ineffectual, dangerous, but in my panic, I will do anything to kill the fear. The buzzing is in my head now, and my skin is itching, crawling with imagined insect legs.

With extraordinary effort, I reach for my phone and look up an exterminator. My fingers can barely dial the numbers in order, but somehow, I get through. As soon as the woman on the other end says "hello" I begin babbling about black locusts.

"They're probably not locusts, sir, not in your pipes."

I can tell they think I'm nuts, but they probably deal with this kind of shit all the time. People are filled with fears, snakes, spiders, rats, all alien to us and our experience. They move, eat, think, reproduce in ways that we can't identify with. We fear the sting or bite of the unknown quantity, something that moves too fast to see, or is comfortable in the dark.

This all happened just a few minutes ago, but I can't make much sense of time right now. They tried to make an appointment for tomorrow, but there's no way this was going to wait. It took everything in me to calm myself, to make my voice drop back to the correct register, to construct sentences that made sense, but because I'm a business owner and deal with the public, they said they could get someone out here in an hour or two. I couldn't wait inside. I told them I'd meet them outside the rear door. Front door was impossible. Someone might see me and ask how I was doing. It was a question I could not answer. I still can't, and I'm writing it out right now, but the words don't exist, as far as I know.

It's cold outside in the alley, and I can't shake the feeling I'm not alone, but I keep telling myself it's just my alley, same place I take my garbage out to every morning, nothing but dumpsters and wooden pallets and a stray cat or dog sometimes. It's better than staying inside. Anything is better than staying inside.

So, the guy shows up. Big guy. White overalls. Utility belt like Batman, covered in all these canisters and tools and things, with a mask dangling around his neck. He shakes my hand and I lead him inside. He asks me all sorts of questions, things about what the bugs looked like, how many there were, the size, shape, color and number. I refuse to go into the bathroom with him at first, but the look he gives me withers my manhood, so I steel myself, and head in.

There is water on the floor around the toilet in the center stall. No evidence of insects, coming out of the commode or otherwise. He checks around the pipes, the drains in the floor, the hand dryers, looks around the baseboards, but there's nothing there.

"What about underneath? You know, the foundation? Maybe there are cracks?" I have to ask. The guy kind of sighs and starts poking around the floor, taking his flashlight and shining it in the darker corners, but finally, he just turns to me and shrugs.

"Well, whatever you saw, it doesn't seem to be here now. I don't see any evidence of roaches, or anything that would indicate a nest. Not even ants. Looks like a pretty clean spot, overall." He stands up and shakes his head.

Desperation claws at my throat. I feel hot. I must be turning red in the face. "What about the dirt underneath this place? Are there a lot of bug problems around here? In the neighborhood?"

He looks at me sideways. "Not really. It's funny though, actually, that you mention it. The soil around here is very heavy in nitrogen. Sometimes that makes plants less resistant to parasites, so under the ideal conditions, this might be a great place for insects."

"Funny, yeah." That's all I can say.

He shakes my hand again and tells me to call him if I see anything else and he'll come by to check it out. He says catch one in a glass or something if I'm able, so I have something to show him. He notices someone's bathroom poetry scrawled beside the toilet and snorts. I look over and don't even crack a smile. It's the classic.

Here I sit all broken hearted

Thought I'd shit, but only farted

Thought I'd take another chance

Tried to fart but shit my pants.

"Poetry, right?" He says, shaking his head.

"Yeah, it's a regular laugh riot. Should have opened a comedy club instead of a bar."

"Maybe so. Who knows?" He says on the way out the door, "Maybe in another world this whole block would be one big insect jungle with no people around at all."

I usher him out and lock the door and stand against it

for several minutes, before I make my way back into the restroom with a mop. I need to clean up the excess water from the floor.

Then, I see the stall door, and I scream. Rage. Fear. The combination of the two. Then, I get my book here, and write it all down. My fingers are squeezing the goddamn pen so hard I think they're about to bleed.

HE WAS WEARING A GRAY SUIT THAT REMINDED ME OF RAIN CLOUDS. HIS BEARD WAS TRIM AND NEAT, SHORTER THAN FATHER'S AND BLACK LIKE A SPADE. HE WORE TINY, CIRCULAR GLASSES THAT MADE HIM LOOK LIKE HE WAS PERPETUALLY SURPRISED. HE SPOKE TO ME IN CALMING TONES, SOFT AND GENTLE. HE KEPT ASKING THE SAME QUESTIONS, AND THEY ALL REVOLVED AROUND MEMORY. WHAT FRAGMENTED IMAGES WERE ETCHED INTO MY

GRAY MATTER, AND WHAT KEY COULD UNLOCK THEM AND LET THEM OUT TO ROAM FREE AGAIN. AS IF THERE WERE SOME KIND OF PUZZLE BOX KEEPING MY MEMORIES INSIDE. AS IF THERE WERE MEANING TO BE FOUND IN OBJECTIVE REALITY AS ANYTHING BEYOND A REFLECTION OF PERCEPTION CROSSED WITH THE STRANGE EFFECTS OF THE MASS HYPNOSIS OF BEING HUMAN.

WE PRETEND THAT WE UNDERSTAND SOMETHING, BUT WE DON'T. THE FRAGILE EGG SHELLS FENCING OFF THIS WORLD FROM THE

NEXT ARE CRACKED AND
BLISTERED, THE YOLKS
SPOTTED WITH BLOOD AND
ROTTING THROUGH.

THE REALITY THIS MAN
WAS SEARCHING FOR
WAS CONNECTED TO MY
MEMORIES OF PAST EVENTS,
AND ALTHOUGH I WAS GOOD
NATURED ENOUGH TO TRY
TO HELP AT FIRST, I QUICKLY
GREW FRUSTRATED WITH
THE IMPOSSIBLE NATURE
OF THE TASK. WHAT GOOD
WERE MEMORIES WHEN A
DIFFERENT ME REMEMBERED
AN ENTIRELY DIFFERENT
ENDING TO EVERY SINGLE
SERIES OF EVENTS?

HE KEPT ASKING ABOUT
DONNIE. SOMETIMES HE
WOULD ASK ABOUT HOW I
HAD LAID MY HANDS ON HER.
IT WAS ALL IN THE ABSTRACT.
I COULD BE A MURDERER OR
A FAITH-HEALER. HER SOFT,
WHITE THROAT MIGHT HAVE
BEEN A STALK OF GRASS,
A TREE TRUNK, OR THE
ANTENNAE OF A BEETLE,
SWIMMING AGAINST RIPPLES
LIKE THEY WERE THE
INCOMING TIDE.

WE TALKED ABOUT MY HANDS.
I COUNTED THE DIGITS. ONE.
TWO. THREE. FOUR. FIVE.

WE PLAYED TOGETHER
THAT DAY. IT WAS A HIKE
ALONG THE RIVER. THERE
WAS NOTHING PLANNED.
NO AGENDA. NO SINISTER
FATE AS PROPHESIED BY
SOME MAGIC FUCKING EIGHT
BALL. IT WAS PLAY. IT WAS
WRESTLING. ROUGHHOUSING.
HIJINKS. TWO CUBS IN THE
ZOO. INNOCENCE. SANCTITY.
PURITY. LIGHT.

SEVENTEEN TIMES. THIS
WAS THE NUMBER OF OUR
VISITATIONS. HOW MANY
TRIPS BACK AND FORTH,
SULKING IN THE BACK SEAT
OF MY PARENTS' SEDAN,
WAITING TO BE EXORCISED
BY THIS STRANGER WITH

THE NEATLY TRIMMED
BEARD AND SPECTACLES.
TO THEM, IT WAS PROGRESS.
TO DONNIE, IT WAS A CHANCE
TO REFLECT AND REGROUP,
AND ALLOWED HER SEED
TO GERMINATE FARTHER
AND FARTHER AWAY FROM
WHERE OUR BLOOD HAD FED
OUR ROOTS.

NOBODY ASKED WHAT IT
WAS TO ME. I TRIED TO
ANSWER THIS FOR MYSELF,
TO COME UP WITH SOME
DESCRIPTIVE WAY TO MAKE
MYSELF UNDERSTAND WHAT
THE PROCESS WAS, WHY
IT WAS, HOW IT MATTERED.
ONE. TWO. THREE. FOUR. I
HID UNDER THE COAT RACK

IN THE HALL CLOSET. THEY FOUND ME. FIVE. SIX. SEVEN. EIGHT. I TRIED TO PRETEND I WAS SICK. DON'T WORRY. HE'S A DOCTOR. THIS WAS A TRICK. A LIE OF THE MIND. A PURGATION OF THE EXCESSES OF LANGUAGE. AN ATROPHY OF TRUST. NINE. TEN. ELEVEN. TWELVE. THE PAPERS SENT HOME HAD OBSCURE AND ESOTERIC SYMBOLS SCRATCHED INTO THEM, DENSE WITH MEANING. I WOULD NOT TAKE MY MEDICATION. I WOULD TRADE IT FOR SANDWICHES IN OTHER KIDS' SCHOOL LUNCHES. I WOULD SELL IT TO THE TEACHER. I WOULD FEED IT TO THE DOG. I WOULD CHOKE ON MY

OWN VOMIT. I WOULD NEVER, EVER CROSS OVER AND IT WOULD NEVER MAKE ANY SENSE.

MY HANDS SHOOK AT NIGHT. I WOULD STARE AT THEM FOR HOURS UNDER THE READING LAMP ON MY HEADBOARD, HIDING UNDER THE COVERS, SHUDDERING, MY NERVES FRAYED LIKE BARE WIRES. WHICH ME WAS I THEN, AND HOW MANY POSSIBILITIES WERE THERE, HURTLING BY ME, UNABLE TO BE SEEN OR CAUGHT? NOBODY COULD TELL ME, AND I COULD TELL NO ONE.

THERE WAS NO JUSTICE. NO MERCY. NO UNDERSTANDING. NO RATIONAL SENSE.

NOTHING BUT INDIFFERENCE.

— DAY 13 —

I got an email from Donnie. The details say it had been sent at two-thirty in the morning. I've been reading it over and over again. I just read it for maybe the twentieth time in a row. I don't know if I should call her again, or just wait it out. I sure as hell don't know what to reply.

```
Hey George—


I wasn't going to email. I still
might not click send on this, but
I'm going to write it out just in
case I get the courage to send it
later.


At first, I was very angry with
you. Nobody has mentioned all that
stuff in years. Not me, not you, not
mom, nobody. And then you bring
it up that casually like that on
the phone? It makes me feel like
you're trying to play some kind of
weird joke. It's not funny, and
it's not cool. If we're going to
talk about that stuff, we can, but
don't pretend it's funny. It nev-
er has been.
```

147

But, the more I thought about it, the more I remember what the doctors said to mom and dad about how there might be some trauma, and that could mean memory problems and stuff later. So, now I'm not sure. I'd like to give you the benefit of the doubt and think that you're actually having some kind of crisis where you really don't remember. Maybe having dreams about it is just a way for the memories to try to signal from behind whatever walls you put up. I don't know.

So I've decided, I'm going to assume the best case scenario and pretend that there's no memory left in your head, and that this doesn't mean much to you beyond a weird dream that you can't seem to make sense of. I guess I have to believe that, because I love you, George, and I don't want this to set back our relationship again. I like having you back in our lives, at least to whatever degree you have been, and if there's some kind of brain issue happening, I want to be there for you, if I can.

The story you mentioned, about following the girl and drowning

her in the river. That's not a
story. You said it was writing
on a wall, but I guess that's
only true if it was written as a
history. That girl was me. That
boy was you. When we were kids,
you tried to drown me in the
river. We had been playing in
the woods and were walking along
the shore when you jumped on me
and pushed me under. I had to
fight you off, but you were getting big, and although I was
still probably as strong as you
then, you had the element of
surprise.

For the first couple of seconds, I was mad, and I remember
I tried to tell you to knock it
off, but when I opened my mouth,
there was river water. I came
up sputtering and took a breath
before you shoved me back under.
Then, I realized your hands were
around my throat and you were
sitting on top of my shoulders.

Mostly I remember the look in
your eyes. We'd always been the
best of friends until then. I
guess I noticed little things.
I think maybe you resented the
fact that I was getting older,
maybe? You never made friends
too easily, not close ones, not

like we were. But there was this
dead zone in your eyes like you
had left the building.

I don't remember exactly how I
got out from under you, but I was
able to squirm far enough to kick
out and up into the air again. I
was coughing up a storm and choking out river water by what felt
like the gallon. I looked back at
you, swearing my head off while
I tried not to choke, and you
were just sitting there. I remember that very well. Just sitting
there in the shallows, looking at
me, but more like looking past me
or through me. It was so weird,
George. I had never seen you look
like that. Not ever. It was like
my little brother got kidnapped
and replaced by a praying man-
tis in the skin of a person. You
weren't really moving, you just
twitched. Like you'd gotten stuck
while playing back a recording of
yourself.

I was scared, George. I was terrified. I backed away and sat down
on the bank a few feet back and
yelled your name. We sat there
like that for probably ten minutes. I was still trying to calm
down and figure out what the hell
was the matter with you. Then all

of the sudden you turned to me and smiled.

You said: "Are you ready to feel the indifference of heaven?"

You wouldn't explain it when I asked what you meant. You just said that and then you kind of shook yourself off, and stood up, and came out of the stream.

I ran, George, and you ran after me, calling out "Donnie, Donnie, Donnie" over and over, screaming. You were scared, I could tell. It was getting dark, but I was so scared of you, and I didn't understand it at all. I didn't have any idea that maybe you didn't understand it either.

We'd already stayed out pretty late. Not a crime, but pushing it a bit, so running through the woods in the dark in a total panic didn't shave off time getting home. By the time I stumbled out of the woods and ran down the street toward our house, all the streetlights had come on.

Mom and dad were relieved to see

us, but they could tell something was immediately wrong. I came up first, panting, out of breath, sopping wet and shuddering. You were following after me still screaming my name, crying and red-faced. I remember them sitting us down and talking to us, asking us what happened, and neither of us could really say. I just kept telling them "George tried to kill me!" They tried asking you what happened, but you wouldn't say anything but my name. They weren't sure if we'd been attacked in the woods, or hurt, or what. Finally, they called the emergency line and a paramedic and a cop car came over, and they talked to us too. Seemed like nobody knew quite what to do, but I remember watching the officer talk to you, and somehow it came out that you had tried to drown me, or yourself, in the river. Maybe it happened, maybe not, nobody could say for sure.

Mom took us to therapy. I got over it, more or less, but you kept going, and the doctor told us all the stuff about how whatever had happened, it was like you were repressing it or something. He said you couldn't admit to trying to hurt me to yourself, and maybe you were traumatized. There was a

bunch of other stuff too… it was
like the memory wasn't there. Like
you hadn't actually done it, but
George, you did. You absolutely
did. There were marks on my neck
and river water in my lungs and
you just went into this delirium
where it was like the whole thing
turned out very differently than
it did.

George, I love you, but if you
remember all this now, after all
these years, you need to tell me.
I'm worried about you. Take care,
okay, and drop me a line once
you've had a chance to think about
all this. We love you.

-Donnie

— DAY 14 —

One black trench coat, size Tall 2XL. 100% leather shell. 100% nylon lining. When dry cleaning is necessary, send to a specialty leather cleaner only.

The mystery of it is in the shadow of it. Just like cartoons. A fake smile.

Look at them, standing on the shoulders of giants, fooling us all into thinking that this is where we started. This is where we ended up. This is a circle. This eats its own tail.

They will hold you under until your scars bloom.

So now I decide, is this my life, or the heap of dirt. Is this the bull or the horn. The rope or the breath. Infinite possibilities and infinite worlds spread before me and all of them rot.

I BREATHE MYSELF IN, ABOVE, THE DARKNESS, THE SYNCHRONICITY OF CHOREOGRAPHED SPACE TRAVEL WITH TIME DILATION.

THERE IS NO NEED FOR A KEY.

THE DOOR IS OPEN.

JUST GO THROUGH IT.

GO THROUGH.

DON'T WORRY ABOUT HEAVEN.

DON'T WORRY ABOUT IT.

DON'T WORRY ABOUT ANYTHING, ANYMORE.

I did NOT write that.
    But here it is. In bold ink.
    It looks like my handwriting.
    On the way out of the bathroom, I happen to glance over at the carving, where someone has chiseled the message "For a bad time, call…" There is a number there. It isn't mine.

I don't memorize numbers anymore, not like I used to back before cell phones and the internet were a thing. I used to know every good friend's phone number by pattern. My fingers would dance around before I ever had to think. Not anymore. Now I need my little electronic address book to reach anyone. Hell, half the time, I forget my own. But this number triggered something. Feels like white hot lightning bursting a string of synapses in the front of my skull.

I can't catch my breath. I hear my heartbeat in my ears, pounding with blood, as I scramble to get my phone out of my pocket. It clatters to the ground, the case popping off the back on impact. The battery explodes out and skids under the sink. I crawl after it, banging my head on the underside of the counter where the sinks are set. The silver pipes swim and twist around as my eyes rattle in their cages. The phone takes far too long to turn back on, after I replace its battery. I squeeze my fingers into a hard fist, until my nails are nearly cutting my palms.

Finally. I fumble and flip to the phone book even before the signal has reconnected. I need to see it for myself, otherwise I'd know this is all in my head.

There it is:

808-555-2827

I looked up at the wall and see it through a swirling, gray haze. The number is the same. For a bad time, call 808-555-2827. It is my sister Donnie's number.

— DAY 15 —

I can't stand it. I'm getting paranoid. I don't even feel comfortable in my own home, which is evidence that I'm completely fucked up. I wish I believed in magic. I'm sure there's salt or some kind of crystals I could spread around, or some form of incense I could burn to purify this place, but I'm stuck with rational thoughts. And those are failing me.

The dreams are terrible. They're making my brain work overtime, sending me horrifying images and messages from my subconscious.

I've had my power drill charging for about twenty minutes. Should be more than enough to do what I need to do. I'm going to open up the crawlspace and convince myself that nothing has changed, and everything is fine.

The damn screws nearly strip when I pull them out of the wood. Looks like they have settled in there pretty well. I'm trying to remember when I put them in, and whether I had any trouble with them then, but it's been too long. It doesn't feel like that long ago though. I keep having these weird deja vu moments where I remember pulling up this trap door and screwing it back again not long ago at all. Feels like last week. But everything is muddy now, and my senses lie to me.

It's dark down there. I've got my flashlight from the other night.

Dust and dirt. Some insulation I store down here. A couple of old wooden picture frames.

I'm going to go down there and see what I can see.

Hopefully, I don't inhale a lungful of black mold spores and choke or find a nest of rats. I'm mostly kidding, but I guess you never know.

I am writing this at twenty minutes past midnight. I'm sorry if the writing is shaky or hard to read. I can't seem to control my fingers very well. I've been shaking like a leaf since I came back up from the crawlspace.

Most of it was empty. Tidy. Nothing disturbed.

Then, I got over to the space right underneath my bedroom at the edge of the house.

I could tell that the dust was disturbed. It looked like drag marks, same as the ones I was leaving behind me as I crawled around down there.

I had the light shining up at the ceiling, which I suppose was really the floor, but, well, above me, anyway. I was following the beam along the seams of the wood, reading over the faded brand logos on the boards and insulation that were still visible, looking for anything out of the ordinary.

At first, I thought it was just a line drawn on the wood from when the place was built that just never got erased, but as my light kept travelling, there were more of them, so I got a closer look.

Dozens of lines, all in neat little rows. Hundreds, maybe. Neatly printed there right above me. I had to flip over on my back to read them.

I was crawling upside-down, backward, shining the light on this scrawl.

CAN'T REMEMBER HOW TO BREATHE

CANT REMEMBER HOW TO
BREATHE

CANT REMEMBER HOW TO
BREATHE

GO DOWNSTAIRS AND VISIT
HER WHERE YOU LEFT HER

SUCH IS THE INDIFFERENCE
OF HEAVEN

PRESS UNTIL THE BUZZING
STOPS

PRESS UNTIL THE BUZZING
STOPS

PRESS UNTIL THE BUZZING STOPS

LIE DOWN AND SLEEP AMONG THE SHEEP

SUCH IS THE INDIFFERENCE OF HEAVEN

It went on like this, and I was reading this garbage and I was backing up. I lurched backward once more, nearing the outside wall of the foundation, and something poked me behind the ear. I reached around and felt for it. Maybe a business card, or a piece of paper, I thought, so I pinched it and pulled it around the front of my face to take a closer look.

It was that damn family photo.

The one from my wallet. The one I lost.

In my mind, there was this picture of me, lying there under the floorboards like I was in my burial plot, instead of flowers I got this picture laying in my folded hands on my chest. I started crying, hot salty tears, and my head began pounding like nothing I've ever felt before. I backed out of there as fast as I could, trying not to brain myself on anything.

As soon as I got out, I didn't even take the time to screw the god damn door shut. I slammed it down and dropped the set of utility shelves in there over top of it. There are cans and tools and all kinds of shit everywhere in there. Who knew what kind of damage I did to the floor. I didn't even care right now. All I knew was, nothing was moving in or out of there until I figured out what was going on.

Checked and double-checked, I knew it was the one from my wallet. I'd seen it a million times. I knew every tiny microscopic bit of wear and tear on each corner, the grain of the photo paper, the feel of it between my fingers, everything.

It was just lying there, face up, right under where I sleep. There are no gaps in the floor, no other access points, no nothing. There is no way that missing photo could have found its way down there. No way, unless someone carried it down and put it there.

— DAY 15 —
— LATE NIGHT —

I can't sleep at home, not after all that. I walk all the way to the bar in the middle of the night. See a few people on the street, and every one of them avoids me. I must look insane. I'm talking to myself, I probably look like shit.

I had to check in there.

Tonight, there is a number underneath "For a bad time, call." It is written in some brownish red dried substance. Blood, shit, I don't know.

It is my phone number, not the bar's but my cell number.

I don't know.

I'm so tired.

I just want to sink into the quiet.

— DAY —

My hand is shaking as I pull it toward me. I cannot open my fingers, cannot let go of the pen. Somewhere, there is some reality in which I can drop the pen. I watch it fall to the tile and roll down the slight incline toward the circular drain in the floor. I wash the graffiti off the stall door and walk out into the bar, and all my friends and family are waiting for me. Everyone is happy to see me, and they cheer and laugh and applaud as I walk into the room. We drink together, and pass the night away, forgetting about ink stained fingertips and memories of a past that never happened.

This is not that reality. Infinite dimensions where this is the side of the coin that landed face up, and infinite dimensions where it was the other side.

In this reality, I slept in the stall last night. I do not remember going to sleep. There is another reality where I'm asleep under the floorboards. Another, where I never woke up at all. Today, I woke up here, already writing, already adding more to the story. There are paragraphs I have no idea about, more about a childhood I do not remember, more about a world in which I am a murderer and where nobody knows me. It flows out of me like history. It may be mine, but I cannot remember it. It happened to a me that isn't me. I am crying, silently. Just a tear from each eye. I feel them run down the sides of my nose. I twitch, slightly. One drop falls and lands on the trembling pen, still writing despite the spasms in my hands.

It won't stop.
It won't stop.
It won't stop.

ABOUT THE AUTHOR

Michael Allen Rose is an author, musician, and performance artist based in Chicago, IL. He works in many genres, including horror, bizarro noir (Embry: Hard Boiled), cartoonish comedy (Party Wolves in My Skull) and experimental and surreal explorations of concepts like gun violence (Boiled Americans). He's been published in anthologies and magazines such as *The Magazine of Bizarro Fiction, Kizuna: Stories for Japan, Fireside Popsicles, Bizarro Bizarro* and *Mighty in Sorrow: A Literary Tribute to David Tibet.* His plays and sketches have been produced and performed in a number of theatres and at Chicago's famed Second City, where he studied in the conservatory program.

Michael also works as a freelance writer and editor and has written everything from descriptions of BDSM equipment to wiki articles on global marijuana legal issues. He hosts the Ultimate Bizarro Showdown at Portland Oregon's "Bizarro Con" each year and he also occasionally performs on stage and does burlesque. He releases industrial and experimental music under the pseudonym Flood Damage. He really likes cats and enjoys good tea and good beer.